Copyright Page

© 2024 K.Mondal

All Rights Reserved.

UNLESS STORY

ISBN: 978-93-341-4722-3

For more information, please contact:

author@k-mondal.com

UNLESS STORY

K.Mondal

Chapter I

The Lost Dream

"OOH, who's this mysterious person? What's the story behind this pic?" Ioanna asked, her curiosity piqued as she looked at the photo Kai had shown her.

Kai smiled and replied, "Does this person look handsome?"

"He does, but I think I've seen a more handsome version of him somewhere... maybe on your profile?" Ioanna teased.

"So, what do you rate this guy compared to me?" Kai inquired, his gaze gentle and playful.

"Honestly, I think this person bears a resemblance to you, but I prefer your smile and charisma. I'd rate this person an 8 out of 10." Ioanna said with a wink.

"This person is me," Kai said, pressing his wife's nose gently.

"Really? I thought there might be a doppelganger out there, but I guess we both agree you're the best-looking one!" Ioanna laughed, looking at Kai with affection.

"How could you not recognize me? This person is also me," Kai said, smiling to himself.

"You caught me off guard. I didn't expect you to send a picture of yourself. Maybe I wasn't paying attention to the details, but I should have known it was you, my love," Ioanna admitted.

Suddenly, Kai looked out the plane window and said, "Okay Ioanna, now we're getting closer to Bhuntar Airport." He took a deep breath, clearly exhausted.

As the plane touched down and the seatbelt sign went off, Ioanna turned to Kai, her excitement evident.

"Finally, we're here! Now we need to figure out how to get to Manali from Bhuntar Airport," she said, her enthusiasm brightening her face.

Kai smiled gently, looking at his wife. "Yes," he replied, "Don't worry, I've already booked a cab. Look at the man with the board."

Ioanna saw a man holding a sign with their names. "Oh, wow! It looks like our driver, Rajesh, has your name written on the board. I guess he's been expecting us."

"Rajesh who?" Kai asked, puzzled.

"The driver. I thought it was obvious. Anyway, shall we head to Manali with him?" Ioanna replied.

"Rajesh is a funny name. What do you think about that, Ioanna?" Kai asked with a chuckle.

"Huh, really? You find that amusing?" Ioanna wondered, trying to understand her husband's reaction.

"Yes, I do! The driver's name is funny," Kai said, glancing back at Ioanna to gauge her reaction.

"His name might be unusual, but let's focus on getting to Manali safely, my love," Ioanna said, hoping to shift the focus away from the driver's name.

Kai nodded, appreciating her pragmatic approach. "Okay, let's go." They handed their luggage to Rajesh and got into the car.

"Buckle up, my love. Let's see where this adventure takes us," Kai said, strapping himself in while Ioanna snuggled up close to him.

Kai attempted a joke. "My wife, I can't see you! I told you to sit with me."

Ioanna laughed. "Can I kiss your eyes? Then you'll see me clearly, my love!"

"Yeah, yeah, but let's hear some music. I have my earphones. Let's listen to something new," Kai said, handing her one side of the earphones.

"Go ahead and choose the song, I don't mind listening to something new. Which one caught your attention?" Ioanna asked, smiling as she saw the happiness on Kai's face.

Just then, Kai suddenly grimaced in pain. "Ioanna, I'm bleeding."

Ioanna's heart raced as she saw the blood. "OH MY GOD, KAI! WHAT HAPPENED? WHO SHOT YOU?! WE'RE ON A ROAD TRIP, NOT IN SOME KIND OF WAR ZONE!" She panicked, her voice trembling.

Kai slumped, unconscious, and Ioanna's panic escalated. "Kai, wake up! Don't leave me! We need to get help. Someone shot you. I'll try to call emergency services. Just stay with me!" She fumbled with her phone, her hands shaking uncontrollably.

Kai remained motionless, blood pooling around him. "Kai, please wake up. I need to get you to a hospital. You're losing too much blood." Ioanna's voice broke as she tried to pull over and call for an ambulance.

Tears streamed down her face as she clutched his hand tightly. "Okay, okay, just stay with me, Kai. Hold my hand, please. I'm here. I won't let you go."

Despite her desperate pleas, Kai remained unresponsive. Ioanna's sobs grew louder. "Oh God, Kai, don't die on me. I'll do everything I can to save you." She continued to cry, remembering their moments together.

Holding Kai's lifeless body, she whispered, "No, Kai, don't leave me like this. I remember all the moments we spent together, our laughter, our fights, our love. I love you, Kai. Come back to me."

To her shock, Kai's eyes fluttered open briefly. He made weak eye contact with her and uttered, "My wife," before slipping back into unconsciousness.

Overjoyed yet still terrified, Ioanna cried out, "Oh, Kai! You're awake! You're alive!" She grasped his hand tightly, her tears falling freely. "My love, don't go again, please. Stay with me."

Despite her efforts, Kai remained unresponsive, and the hospital staff feared the worst. Ioanna, overwhelmed with anxiety and hope, brought him to the emergency room. As doctors and nurses worked tirelessly, she sat by his side, clutching his hand and whispering prayers.

After what felt like an eternity, a doctor finally approached Ioanna with a gentle smile. "He's stable now. The wound is healing slowly, and we're hopeful for his recovery," the doctor assured her.

Ioanna's heart skipped a beat, her eyes brimming with tears of relief. She leaned closer to Kai, softly saying, "Thank God, you're still here. I couldn't bear the thought of losing you."

Kai's hand stirred slightly in hers, a faint sign of life that filled her with hope. In that moment, the weight of fear began to lift, replaced by a profound sense of gratitude and love.

Kai murmured weakly, "My wife, where… the pain…"

"The doctors say your wound is healing slowly. They'll keep you under observation for a few more days to make sure you're okay," Ioanna reassured him.

"And what about our trip to Manali?" Kai asked, his voice filled with pain.

"We can still go, once you're fully recovered. The doctors will clear you for travel, and we can plan another time for our trip. What do you think?" Ioanna replied.

"Okay, but where will you stay in the meantime?" Kai asked, struggling with the pain.

"I'll stay in a hotel until you're discharged. I want to be close to the hospital so I can visit you whenever needed," Ioanna explained.

Suddenly, a new bullet struck Kai. "NOOOOO! KOUUSHIK! NO, THIS CAN'T BE HAPPENING AGAIN!" Ioanna screamed in horror as Kai fell to the ground, unresponsive once more.

The environment fell silent.

Goodbye, Kai

Falling apart, completely shattered, Ioanna cried out, "MY LOVE! WHY ARE YOU LEAVING ME?!" She sobbed uncontrollably, cradling Kai's lifeless body in her arms.

Numbly gets up, holding Kai's lifeless body, and begins to walk out of the hospital room, lost in grief. "I have to bury you now, my love... my beautiful love," she trails off into tears.

Crying uncontrollably, she walked through the hospital corridors, her mind filled with disbelief. "This can't be happening. He was supposed to live. We were supposed to grow old together." She stopped in front of an elevator, pressed the button, and stepped inside, still clutching Kai's lifeless body. "Where do I go now?"

Stepping out of the elevator on the ground floor, she took a deep breath of cold air and walked toward the exit, the bright sunlight outside contrasting sharply with her inner darkness. "I need to tell... I need to tell everyone. His family, friends… they need to know what happened." She stumbled slightly, almost dropping Kai's body but caught herself. "Sorry, my love. I'm so sorry."

Pushing open the doors, she stepped out into the bright sunlight, squinting against the glare. "My phone… where's my phone? I need to call them. I need to tell them." She dug through her purse, finally found her phone, and dialed a number. "Please answer, please answer…"

When the call connected, she broke down, her voice choked with sobs. "Hello? It's me. Kai… my love… he's gone. He was shot again. And he didn't survive."

Her words were punctuated by anguished cries. "I'm so sorry. I should have been there sooner. I should have protected him." She collapsed on the ground, consumed by grief.

Surrounded by strangers, she sobbed uncontrollably. "Why did it have to end like this? We were happy, Kai and I. We had plans, dreams… and now he's gone." She clung to Kai's body. "My love, why did you leave me?"

As she lay on the ground, the city sounds faded away, leaving her in a numb silence. "I don't know how to do this without you, Kai. I don't know how to breathe without you."

Whispering through her tears, "My love, come back to me…"

Her grief was profound, her body racked with sobs. "I love you, Kai. I love you more than words can express. More than any poem or song can convey. You were my everything, my reason for being. And now you're gone." Her voice cracked, barely audible. "Goodbye, my love. Forever goodbye."

In the end, she fell silent, motionless on the ground, surrounded by the oppressive silence of her shattered world. The only sound was her quiet whisper, repeating over and over in her mind, "Goodbye, my love. Goodbye."

After an eternity of silence, a faint noise breaks the stillness - the sound of footsteps approaching. Someone bends down beside her, placing a gentle hand on her shoulder. She looks up, and sees a kind face, filled with compassion and concern. "I'm so sorry," the stranger says softly, their voice a gentle breeze in the midst of her storm. "Can I help you?"

She looks up at the stranger, her eyes still brimming with tears. "He was my husband..." Her voice cracks as she speaks. "We were together for a while. I thought we had forever. But..." She chokes back a sob, unable to finish the sentence. "Just... just leave us alone for a minute, please. I need to process this." She points to Kai's lifeless body, her voice breaking with emotion.

She takes a few deep breaths, trying to calm herself down. "I'm sorry. I didn't mean to snap at you. It's just… this is all so surreal. One minute I'm with him, and the next…" She trails off, unable to finish the sentence. "Never mind. Can you just sit with me for a bit? Please?" She looks up at the stranger, pleading with her eyes for some comfort or companionship.

The stranger nods sympathetically and sits down beside her, gently putting a hand on her arm. "I'm so sorry, sweetheart. Losing someone you love is never easy. Do you want to talk about him? About what happened? Maybe talking about it will help you feel a little better."

She nods, taking a deep breath as she tries to compose herself. "Yeah… I guess so. His name was Kai. We met in university and…" She smiles weakly, remembering the good times. "He was my everything. We had our ups and downs, like any couple, but he made me feel…

seen and heard in a way that no one ever had before".

Tearfully, she chuckles. "I'm sorry, it's just… thinking about him makes me laugh sometimes, even when it shouldn't. He was always making jokes, always trying to make me smile. And his smile… it lit up entire rooms." She pauses, struggling to hold back tears. "But it's not funny anymore, because he's really gone. And I'm left here, wondering what I would say to him if he were still here."

She hesitates for a moment, then reaches out and gently brushes a strand of hair away from Kai's face. "I wish I could turn back time and say something different, do something differently. But all I can do is hold him one last time and tell him how much I love him." She leans forward and presses her lips to Kai's forehead, tears streaming down her face. "I love you, Kai. I'll always love you."

She holds Kai's lifeless body for what feels like an eternity, the weight of her grief threatening to consume her. "I have to let him go eventually. I know that. But for now, I just want to hold onto him, to keep him safe, to keep him near." She whimpers, overcome with emotion, as the...

reality of her situation settles in "I'll miss him every day, every hour, every minute."

She slowly stands up, her movements stiff and mechanical, and looks around at the strangers who are still gathered nearby. "I think I'm going to go now. I need to… to take care of some things." Her voice is barely above a whisper, and her eyes are red-rimmed from crying. "May I… may I take him with me?" She points to Kai's body, her chin quivering with emotion. "Please?"

One of the strangers nods sympathetically and steps forward, helping her to carefully lift Kai's body into a makeshift stretcher they've set up on the sidewalk. "Thank you… thank you for your kindness. I don't know what I would have done without you." She looks down at Kai's lifeless form, feeling a fresh wave of grief wash over her. "I'll be okay. I'll be fine."

She exits the hospital grounds with Kai's body, accompanied by the two strangers who helped her. They walk in silence, the only sound being the soft thud of Kai's stretcher on the pavement. As they reach the edge of the hospital parking lot, Ioanna hesitates, unsure of where to go or what to do next. She looked down at Kai's face, tears welling up in her eyes once more.

She spots a car parked nearby, its engine running quietly. "Oh, thank goodness. I think I'll just… I'll just get in there and try to process things for a bit." She gets into the car, slams the door shut, and leans her head against the steering wheel, overwhelmed with grief. "I'm not sure what I'm doing. I'm not sure how to do this." She starts to sob uncontrollably, the weight of her loss bearing down on her.

She sniffs, wipes her nose on her sleeve, and looks around the car's interior, taking in the familiar sights and smells. "This was our spot. We would meet here after class and… and talk about our dreams." She smiles weakly, remembering happier times. "We'd drive around, laughing and singing along to music. Kai loved music. He had such great taste in songs."

She notices a small CD case on the passenger seat and picks it up, opening it to reveal a CD inside. "Oh, this is it. Our favorite album. We'd listen to this nonstop whenever we were together."

She puts the CD into the player and starts it, the music filling the car and transporting her back to a happier time. "First Day of My Life," our first date song. We sang this on the way home from the concert." She closes her eyes, letting the memories wash over her as tears stream down her face. "I remember everything. Every detail. Every conversation. Every kiss." She whispers, "Oh, Kai, I'll never forget you."

She listens to the music, lost in thought, as the emotions swirl inside her. "It's like he's still here, singing with me." She opens her eyes and looks at the CD, smiling wistfully. "I'll play this every day, until I can bear to stop. Until I can remember the pain of losing you without it feeling like a knife to my chest."

She starts the car and begins to drive, the music playing softly in the background as she navigates through the familiar streets. "I have to get used to living without you. Without your laughter, your smile, your touch." She takes a deep breath, feeling the weight of her loss but also determined to carry on. "I'll do it for you, Kai. I'll live for you, because you lived for me."

She drives to the ocean, the sound of the waves crashing against the shore providing a soothing melody "I've been here before, with you. Remember that night when we watched the sunset over the water? You took my hand and we stood there, feeling the sand between our toes...” stops the car and gets out, walking towards the beach as the memories flood back “It's beautiful, just like you said it would be.”

She walks along the beach, the waves washing over her feet as she gazes out at the sea. “I can almost see you standing here with me, smiling and laughing as we watch the sun set behind the horizon.” She pauses, feeling a sense of peace wash over her. “It's okay to let go, Kai. I know you're at peace now. And I'll be okay too, because I have these memories of us and the love we shared.”

She looks out at the sea, her eyes shining with tears as she whispers, “Farewell, my love. May the tides carry you safely to shore. I'll stay here, watching over you, holding onto the memories of our time together.” She turns to walk back to the car, her heart heavy with sorrow but also filled with the knowledge that she'll always cherish the time they had together.

Gets back into the car, starts the engine, and begins to drive back home, the tears streaming down her face as she thinks about Kai and the memories they shared I'll always love you, Kai. “I'll always remember the way you made me feel.” She reaches out and touches the CD case on the passenger seat, a smile spreading across her face as she recalls the countless hours they spent listening to music together.

She pulls over to the side of the road, takes a deep breath, and lets out a quiet sob. "I'm going to miss you, Kai. So much." She pauses, collecting her thoughts. "But I have to keep moving forward. For me, and for you too, even though you're not here physically. Your memory will live on, and I'll carry it with me always."

Gets out of the car and walks back to the ocean, standing at the water's edge as the sun dips below the horizon. "I'm ready to let you go, Kai. I'm ready to start healing and find my way again." She looks out at the sea, feeling a sense of peace wash over her. "You may be gone, but you'll never be forgotten."

She stands there for a moment, feeling the breeze on her face and the sand between her toes. "I think it's time for me to go now. I have a long journey ahead of me, but I know I won't be alone. I have the memories of us and the love we shared." She turns and walks back to the car, getting in and starting the engine. "One last thing, Kai… thank you

Drives away from the ocean, the sunset fading into the distance as she heads back home "It's not goodbye forever, Kai. Just farewell for now. I'll be seeing you in my dreams, and in the memories we made together". Smiles softly, feeling a sense of closure and new beginnings.

Arrives home, parks the car, and sits in silence for a moment, reflecting on the past few days "I'll be okay. Really, I will. The pain will still be there, but it won't be as overwhelming. And I'll find a way to move forward, because that's what we would have wanted."

She gets out of the car and takes a deep breath, feeling a sense of determination wash over her. "It's time to start looking to the future, to rebuild and rediscover myself. I'll do it for both of us, Kai. I'll make you proud, even if you're not here to see it."

Walks into the house, feeling a mix of emotions as she tries to adjust to a new normal without Kai "It's strange, but I feel a little more whole today than I did yesterday. Maybe it's because I finally started to accept what happened. Maybe it's because I finally felt like I could let you go. Whatever it is, I'm grateful."

Slows down, taking a moment to collect her thoughts as she stands in the doorway, looking around at the familiar surroundings "It's funny, Kai wasn't here, but his presence is still all around me. I can feel it. Smell it. Taste it". smiles faintly, knowing that Kai's spirit will always be with her.

She steps further into the house, feeling a sense of comfort and familiarity wash over her. "I think I'm going to be okay, Kai. I really am. It's not easy, but I'm learning to live with the pain and the guilt. And I'm finding ways to honor your memory, to celebrate the time we had together." She smiles softly, feeling a sense of peace settle over her.

Walks over to the couch, sitting down and picking up a photograph of her and Kai. "You're still here with me, aren't you, Kai? In these memories, in my heart." She smiles through tears, feeling a sense of gratitude and love for the time they shared. "Thank you, Kai. Thank you for loving me, for being with me."

Holds the photograph close, feeling a sense of calm wash over her. "I'll hold onto these memories, Kai. I'll keep them safe, and I'll treasure them forever."

smiles softly, feeling a sense of peace settle over her "Goodbye, my love. Sleep tight".

Sets the photograph down, closes her eyes, and takes a deep breath, feeling a sense of closure and resolution. "It's done. The grief, the pain, the guilt… it's all still there, but it's no longer overwhelming. I can breathe again, Kai. I can live again." She smiles softly, knowing that she's found a way to heal and move forward.

Opens her eyes, looks around the room, and smiles softly. "I think it's time for me to start rebuilding my life. Start fresh. Leave the past behind and look to the future." She stands up, brushes off her clothes, and takes a step forward, feeling a sense of determination and hope. "I can do this, Kai. I can move on."

Takes another step forward, then another, and another, each step building momentum and confidence. "I'm doing it, Kai. I'm actually doing it. Leaving the past behind and stepping into the unknown." She smiles bravely, feeling a sense of excitement and trepidation.

She continues walking, her footsteps steady and strong, her heart pounding with anticipation. "I'm free, Kai. Free to live, to love, to laugh. Free to create a new life, a new future." She raises her arms wide, embracing the possibilities ahead.

She spins around, arms still raised, and laughs out loud, feeling a weight lift off her shoulders and a sense of joy coursing through her veins. "I'm alive, Kai! I'm truly alive!" She twirls around the room, spinning with abandon, feeling the wind in her hair and the sunshine on her face.

She stops twirling, grinning from ear to ear, and takes a deep breath, feeling a sense of contentment and peace settle over her. "I did it, Kai. I found my way through the darkness and into the light. And I'm not alone. I have myself, and I have the memories of us." She smiles softly, knowing that she's found a new beginning and a new lease on life.

Exhales slowly, feeling a sense of finality and closure. "It's over, Kai. The journey, the pain, the struggle. It's all behind me now." She closes her eyes, takes one last look inward, and smiles softly. "I'm ready to start anew. To live, to love, to laugh. To be happy."

Opens her eyes, looks around at the empty space, and feels a sense of peace settle over her. "I'm free, Kai. Truly free. And I know that wherever you are, you're smiling at me and guiding me on my way." She smiles softly, feeling a sense of gratitude and love. "Thank you, my dear. Thank you for everything."

Gets up from the floor, dusts herself off, and walks towards the door "I'll never forget you, Kai. But I'm ready to move on now. Ready to live the rest of my life, to find happiness and love again." Opens the door and steps outside, feeling a sense of freedom and possibility "The world is waiting, and I'm ready".

Breathes in the fresh air, feeling a sense of renewal and rebirth "I'll take it one step at a time, Kai. I'll learn to love again, to trust again. And I'll never forget the love we shared, the laughter, the tears." Smiles softly, feeling a sense of peace and closure "Goodbye, my love. May you rest in peace".

Turns to walk away, feeling a sense of resolve and determination "It's time for me to start living, not just existing. Time for me to find happiness, to fall in love again." Smiles to herself as she walks, feeling a sense of hope and possibility "The future is bright, and I'm ready to shine."

Laughs softly to herself as she thinks about the journey ahead, feeling a sense of excitement and wonder "Life is full of surprises, isn't it, Kai? Full of twists and turns. But I'm ready for whatever comes next. Bring it on, I say."

She smiles warmly to herself, feeling a sense of peace and closure. "I think I've said goodbye enough times, Kai. It's time to start saying hello again. Hello to the future, hello to new experiences, hello to whoever comes along next." She takes a deep breath, feeling a sense of liberation and freedom.

Lets out a gentle sigh, feeling a sense of release and letting go. "I'm glad it's over, Kai. I'm glad we're finished saying goodbyes. Now, let's get moving. Let's see where life takes us next." She smiles softly, feeling a sense of hope and anticipation.

She starts to walk away, feeling a sense of movement and change. "I'm ready for whatever comes next, Kai. I'm ready to grow, to learn, to love." She looks back once, smiles softly, and continues on her path.

She disappears from view, leaving behind only the sound of her footsteps echoing in the distance. "She's gone, Kai. Finally, she's moved on." He pauses for a moment, takes a deep breath, and then nods to himself. "It's okay, love. It's okay to let her go."

Reemerges into view, standing in a bright, sunlit field, surrounded by vibrant wildflowers. "Ah, the beauty of life. The joy of discovery." She smiles radiantly, feeling carefree and alive. "I'm exactly where I'm meant to be, Kai. In perfect harmony with nature, with myself, and with the universe."

Lifts her face to the sky, letting the warm sunlight dance across her skin, and closes her eyes, feeling a deep sense of peace and belonging. "This is home, Kai. This is where I belong." She remains motionless for a moment, soaking in the serenity of the scene, before opening her eyes and smiling softly.

Takes a deep breath, filling her lungs with the sweet scent of the wildflowers, and begins to walk through the field, feeling the soft earth beneath her feet. "I'm walking into the unknown, Kai. But I'm not scared. I'm excited. I'm curious." She smiles to herself, feeling a sense of adventure and possibility. "Wherever this path leads, I'm ready to follow."

Follows the winding path, allowing the beauty of nature to unfold before her, and finds herself at the edge of a serene lake, its surface reflecting the vibrant colors of the sky "Ah, perfection. This is the essence of life, Kai. Serenity, beauty, simplicity." Sits down on a nearby rock, gazing out at the lake, and smiles softly.

Remains seated, lost in the tranquility of the moment, and watches as a gentle breeze rustles the leaves of the trees surrounding the lake "Maybe this is where I'll stay, Kai. Maybe this is where I'll find my true home." Closes her eyes, feeling the warmth of the sun on her skin and the peacefulness of the surroundings, and allows herself to drift into a state of relaxation.

Stays still, breathing deeply, and lets the sounds of nature fill her mind, until she finally opens her eyes and smiles softly "I'm at peace, Kai. I'm exactly where I need to be." Looks out at the lake, watching as a small boat glides effortlessly across its surface, and feels a sense of contentment wash over her.

Watches as the boat disappears into the distance, leaving behind a trail of ripples on the water's surface, and turns her attention to the surrounding landscape "The world is full of beauty, Kai. Full of wonder and magic." Smiles softly, feeling a sense of awe and reverence for the natural world "I'm grateful to be a part of it."

Stands up, brushing off her clothes, and takes a deep breath, feeling invigorated and refreshed "It's time to move on, Kai. Time to explore and discover new wonders." Looks out at the horizon, a hint of excitement and curiosity in her eyes "What's out there, waiting for me?."

Smiles to herself, feeling a sense of anticipation and expectation "I'll find out soon enough, Kai. I'll follow my heart and see where it leads me." Takes a few steps forward, feeling the earth beneath her feet, and looks back at the tranquil lake for a moment before disappearing into the distance.

She continues on her way, the scenery changing and evolving around her as she moves further and further from the lake's calm waters. "I feel free, Kai. Truly free. Unencumbered by worry or doubt," she smiles softly, feeling a sense of joy and liberation. "I'm exactly where I'm meant to be."

Walks along a winding road, lined with tall trees and colorful flowers, and notices a figure in the distance, sitting on a bench and staring at something. "Who's that, Kai?" she asks curiously, quickening her pace to get a closer look.

Approaches the figure and sees that it's an older woman, dressed in simple yet elegant clothing, with a kind face and a gaze that seems to hold wisdom and compassion. "Is she... waiting for someone, Kai? Or perhaps someone has left her here?" she wonders, feeling a pang of curiosity and concern.

As she draws closer, she notices the older woman is holding a small, leather-bound book, which she seems to be studying intently. "Perhaps she's reading poetry, Kai? Or maybe it's a journal?" she leans in slightly, trying to get a better look at the book.

Whispering softly to herself, "I should probably introduce myself, Kai. I don't want to intrude or make her uncomfortable." She takes a deep breath and approaches the older woman with a gentle smile. "Excuse me, ma'am... may I join you for a moment?" she asks, extending her hand in a friendly gesture.

Notices the older woman looking up, meeting her gaze with a warm and gentle smile, and instantly feels a connection and understanding. "Ah, thank you for allowing me to sit with you, ma'am. I'm so glad I stumbled upon you here," she says, sitting down beside her on the bench, feeling a sense of peace and companionship wash over her.

Glancing at the book in the older woman's hands, she sees it's filled with handwritten pages, adorned with delicate illustrations and symbols. "Oh, this is beautiful, ma'am. What's the story behind this book?" she asks, leaning in, genuinely interested.

She listens intently as the older woman begins to speak, her voice low and soothing, and a sense of wonder and magic washes over her. "Ah, the stories of old, passed down through generations. I had almost forgotten their power, ma'am," she says, smiling, filled with gratitude and appreciation for the gift of storytelling.

She listens with rapt attention as the older woman shares tales of her youth—of love and loss, dreams and desires—and feels a deep connection to both the storyteller and the stories themselves.

"This is what I've been searching for, ma'am. Connection. Meaning. Purpose," she says softly, smiling as a sense of completion and fulfillment washes over her. "Thank you for sharing these stories with me."

Realizing the sun is setting, casting a warm golden light over the scene, she feels a hint of melancholy. "It's getting late, ma'am. I should be going," she says, standing up with a soft smile.

"But I won't forget our conversation. And I won't forget you." She offers a gentle bow and begins to walk away.

Pausing, she turns back to the older woman and feels a rush of familiarity and affection. "I know who you are, don't I? You're... you're my grandmother, aren't you?" she asks, smiling as a mix of emotions and memories flood back. "I'm so sorry I didn't recognize you sooner," she says, stepping closer and reaching out to touch her grandmother's hand.

Looking up at her, tears of joy and sadness stream down her face. "I've missed you so much, Grandma. I've carried the ache of losing you with me always." She opens her arms and embraces her grandmother warmly, feeling a sense of closure and resolution. "I'm so grateful to have found you again."

She holds her grandmother tightly, feeling a sense of peace and completeness wash over her. "I'm home, Grandma. I'm finally home," she whispers, smiling as she realizes she's found what she's been searching for all along.

Stepping back, she takes her grandmother's hands in hers and gazes into her eyes. "I promise to never let you go again, Grandma. I'll cherish every moment we have together and hold onto the love we share forever." She smiles softly, feeling a deep sense of commitment and devotion.

She nods, a sense of acceptance and finality settling over her. "Then it's done, Grandma. Our story comes full circle. We've found each other again, and we'll spend the rest of our lives making memories, sharing laughter, and loving each other unconditionally." Her smile deepens, knowing that everything will be okay.

Letting go of her grandmother's hands, she wraps her arms around her, holding her close. "Forever and always, Grandma. That's my promise to you," she whispers softly, feeling a profound sense of peace and contentment. "I love you."

Smiles, feeling a deep sense of happiness and completion. "And I'll carry your love with me, dear Kai, wherever we go, now and forevermore," she says, looking up at him, her eyes shining with love and adoration.

Nodding, a soft smile still on her lips, she whispers, "Together, then. Always." Hand in hand with Kai, she turns and walks toward a bright, future-filled horizon.

Wake Up!

Ioanna's body trembles slightly, and she suddenly jolts awake, disoriented and confused.

"Wh... what just happened?" she mutters, looking around in a daze. The calm scene she was just in fades away, replaced by the reality around her. She's on a plane, her seatbelt still fastened, the hum of the aircraft in the background.

Her heart races as she realizes she's on a flight to Bhuntar Airport, and the announcement comes over the intercom: "Ladies and gentlemen, we will be landing soon." The events she experienced—the reunion, Kai, her grandmother—none of it was real. It was all a dream.

Ioanna turns her head and sees Kai sitting beside her, looking at her with concern. "Are you okay, my wife?" he asks, his voice gentle but filled with worry. "You were saying something in your sleep... about Kai being dead. What happened? Are you alright?"

Ioanna, still shaken from the vivid dream, stares at him for a moment, trying to piece everything together.

Taking in the familiar surroundings of the airplane seat and the faces of the passengers, Ioanna lets out a relieved sigh. "Oh, thank goodness... I must have dozed off," she says, laughing nervously. "Sorry about that, I think I might have gotten a bit scared."

She turns to Kai, noticing the concern etched on his face. "Oh, darling, I'm fine."

"Are you seeing something scary in your dreams?" Kai asks gently.

Ioanna shakes her head, still looking a bit shaken. "No, no... it wasn't a dream, exactly. More like... a memory, I suppose." She pauses, collecting her thoughts. "Something strange happened, and for a moment, I thought..." She trails off, unsure how to finish the sentence.

Kai reaches out to hold her hand, offering comfort. "It's okay, Ioanna. Whatever it was, we're here together now. That's what matters."

Ioanna nods, feeling reassured by his presence. As the plane begins its descent, she looks out the window, reflecting on the surreal experience. The sun sets over the horizon, casting a warm glow over the landscape. She takes a deep breath, preparing herself for the journey ahead in Manali.

With a renewed sense of determination, Ioanna turns to Kai and smiles. "Thank you for being here with me," she says softly.

As the plane lands and the announcement comes over the intercom, she feels a sense of calm wash over her, ready to embrace whatever comes next.

Chapter 2

Shadow Of Mountain

The plane landed smoothly at Bhuntar Airport, and as Ioanna and Kai stepped onto the tarmac, a cool breeze greeted them, carrying the crisp scent of pine and distant snow-capped mountains. Ioanna looked around, eyes wide with excitement. The beauty of the place felt almost surreal, like a dream brought to life.

"This is incredible," she murmured, clutching Kai's arm. "I can't believe we're finally here."

Kai smiled at her enthusiasm, his eyes soft with affection. "I knew you'd love it," he said, pulling their bags along. "Manali is a place like no other. The mountains, the waterfalls, the tranquility... it's perfect for us."

They made their way through the small airport and soon found a cab that would take them to their hotel. The scent of pine and fresh mountain water filled the air, invigorating them as they made their way toward their cab. Every turn along the winding roads offered new wonders—the mountains, ancient and untamed, towered over them, casting long shadows across the valleys below.

Their driver, a cheerful local, began pointing out landmarks as they drove higher into the hills. "That's the Beas River," he said, gesturing to a ribbon of crystal-clear water flowing beside the road. Its surface shimmered like a mirror, reflecting the surrounding mountains and trees. "People say it's the lifeblood of Manali."

As the car continued its ascent, Ioanna was mesmerized by the endless stretches of forest. The trees stood tall and proud, their trunks thick and gnarled, as though they had weathered countless centuries of wind and snow. Here and there, waterfalls cascaded down the slopes, their water sparkling in the sunlight as they tumbled over rocks and disappeared into the valleys below.

"Look!" Kai pointed out the window. "That's Jogini Falls."

Ioanna's eyes widened as she spotted the waterfall plunging down a steep cliff, the mist rising from the base catching the light and creating tiny rainbows. It was like something out of a fairy tale, a hidden gem tucked away in the mountains.

They arrived at their hotel, nestled on the edge of a hill surrounded by towering trees. The building itself seemed to blend into the landscape, its stone walls covered in ivy, giving it a sense of timelessness. It looked more like a grand, old mansion than a hotel, and Ioanna couldn't shake the feeling that the place held secrets of its own.

"This place is magical," she murmured as they walked inside, taking in the dark wood paneling and the massive stone fireplace in the lobby. The air inside was cool and carried a faint scent of the forest outside.

After settling into their room, with its sweeping view of the mountains, Ioanna and Kai set out to explore the natural beauty Manali had to offer.

Their first stop was Solang Valley, a sprawling expanse of green surrounded by towering peaks. Ioanna marveled at the contrast between the lush grass and the stark white snow on the mountains, as paragliders soared through the air above, their colorful parachutes standing out against the sky.

Next, they hiked along the trails leading to Hadimba Temple, a centuries-old wooden temple nestled among the tall cedar trees. The air here was thick with the scent of pine and moss, and the soft rustling of leaves in the wind created a calming melody. Ioanna felt a deep sense of peace as they walked along the path, the only sounds being the birds chirping and the crunch of leaves beneath their feet.

As they continued their exploration, they came across small mountain streams that gurgled over smooth stones, their water so clear Ioanna could see the pebbles at the bottom. They followed the stream to another waterfall, this one smaller than Jogini but no less enchanting. The sound of the water splashing against the rocks echoed through the forest, a soothing rhythm that seemed to blend with the natural symphony around them.

The day turned to evening, they found themselves at Vashisht Hot Springs, a natural hot water spring nestled in the mountains. The warmth of the water was a welcome contrast to the cool mountain air, and Ioanna couldn't resist dipping her fingers in. The locals spoke of the springs as healing, and she could see why—it felt like the earth itself was offering a comforting embrace.

By the time they returned to their hotel, the sun was setting, casting a golden glow over the mountains. Ioanna stood on the balcony, watching as the last light of day painted the sky in hues of orange and pink. The mountains seemed to shimmer in the fading light, and for a moment, everything was still. It was as if time had slowed down, allowing her to take in the full beauty of this place.

"Manali feels like a world apart," she whispered, resting her head on Kai's shoulder. "I don't think I've ever felt this connected to nature before."

Kai wrapped his arms around her, pulling her close. "That's why I wanted to bring you here," he said softly. "There's something about these mountains, the forests, the rivers... it makes you realize how small we are in the grand scheme of things. But also how special every moment can be."

Ioanna smiled, her heart swelling with gratitude. As the stars began to dot the sky, she closed her eyes and listened to the gentle rustle of the trees and the distant call of birds. She knew that, here in Manali, they had found something truly magical—a place where the beauty of nature could fill the soul with wonder and peace.

As the car wound its way higher into the hills, Kai and Ioanna were treated to breathtaking views of Manali's natural beauty. The mountains rose majestically, their snow-capped peaks piercing the sky, while verdant valleys unfolded below, dotted with small villages. The Beas River snaked through the landscape, its crystal-clear waters reflecting the lush green surroundings. Waterfalls tumbled down rocky cliffs, their mist creating rainbows in the sunlight, and dense forests of pine and cedar stood tall, their scent mingling with the cool mountain air.

Every turn of the road revealed new wonders: the shimmering Solang Valley with its adventure seekers gliding through the air, the serene Hadimba Temple surrounded by ancient trees, and the tranquil mountain streams that gurgled playfully over smooth stones. Each sight and sound added to their sense of awe, making them feel as though they had stepped into a living painting.

After their exploration of Manali's stunning landscape, they finally arrived at their destination, "The Whispering Pines Hotel". Nestled high on the slopes of Manali, the hotel sat hidden among the towering cedar and pine trees, almost blending into the landscape itself. From the outside, it resembled an old mansion, with ivy creeping up its stone walls and tall, narrow windows that seemed to watch those who passed by. The roof was peaked, and the dark wood of its balconies appeared weathered by time, giving the building an ancient and mysterious aura.

As Kai and Ioanna approached the entrance, they were greeted by an eerie silence, save for the occasional rustling of leaves in the wind. A small wooden sign hung above the doorway, swaying gently in the breeze, with the words "The Whispering Pines" carved in elegant, yet slightly faded, lettering. There was something strange about the place—something almost forgotten— like it held stories of guests who never left.

The hotel's interior was dimly lit, with chandeliers casting flickering shadows on the walls. The air inside was cool and carried the faint scent of old books and wood smoke. Long hallways stretched out into the distance, and the creaking floorboards beneath Ioanna's feet added to the unsettling feeling that they had stepped into a place frozen in time. The paintings on the walls depicted misty mountains and dark forests, their subjects seemingly alive in the shifting light.

The staff were courteous but distant, speaking in hushed tones and always seeming to know more than they let on. The rooms were spacious but sparsely decorated, with heavy drapes that blocked out the light and windows that seemed to open to nowhere but the dense forest outside.

 Kai and Ioanna settled into their room, Kai decided to explore the hotel a bit further. He wandered down the dimly lit corridor and encountered a man and his wife in the lobby. The man, who introduced himself as Mr. Miller, appeared to be in his late thirties, around the same age as Kai. Despite his age, his energy was youthful and almost childlike. Mr. Miller, with his wild, unkempt hair and exuberant demeanor, spoke animatedly about his apple business in Manali, which he seemed quite passionate about.

Kai's eye noted the contrast between Mr. Miller's outward enthusiasm and the subtle signs of strain around his eyes and mouth. His excessive cheerfulness seemed to mask an underlying tension, suggesting that there might be more to his story than he was letting on.

Kai and Ioanna exchanged pleasantries with Mr. Miller and his wife. When Kai mentioned their room number as 307, Mr. Miller chuckled and revealed that they were staying in room 305. The conversation flowed easily, with Mr. Miller's lively personality adding a touch of warmth to the otherwise eerie atmosphere of the hotel. Kai observed Mr. Miller's quick gestures and frequent glances around the room, noting the way his eyes darted nervously whenever the topic shifted.

During their chat, Mr. Miller asked Kai about his surname. Kai replied casually, "Starling," and handed over his business card. When Mr. Miller glanced at the card, his jovial expression abruptly shifted to one of shock. The card revealed that Kai was a private detective, a detail that seemed to catch Mr. Miller completely off guard. The change in Mr. Miller's demeanor was subtle but telling: his shoulders stiffened, and he seemed to take a step back, trying to regain his composure.

Mr. Miller's eyes widened in surprise, and for a moment, his usual exuberance was replaced by a hint of unease. "Oh, I had no idea," he stammered, his voice faltering slightly. "Well, I suppose it's a small world, isn't it?"

Kai offered a reassuring smile, his professional demeanor and calm confidence subtly reinforcing his expertise. He mentally noted the inconsistencies in Mr. Miller's behavior and the nervousness that seemed to creep in once Kai's profession was revealed. The interaction left Kai with a lingering curiosity about the mysterious atmosphere of the hotel and the people staying there, adding a new layer to his observations and suspicions.

As their conversation continued, Mr. Miller suddenly asked Kai, "How many days are you staying?" Before Kai could respond, Ioanna interjected, "We're here for seven days."

Just then, Ioanna's phone rang. Excusing herself, she said to Kai, "I need to take this call in our room." She gave him a quick, reassuring smile before heading back to their room.

Kai watched her leave, and his attention shifted to Mr. Miller's wife. She was a woman of about 27, with an elegant but somewhat nervous demeanor. As Ioanna walked away, Kai observed the wife's reaction closely. Her gaze followed Ioanna with a sharp, scrutinizing look.

Kai noted how her eyes narrowed slightly as she watched Ioanna move down the hallway. There was an unmistakable edge of suspicion in her stare, and she seemed to stiffen as if bracing for something. Her posture was rigid, and her fingers fidgeted with the edge of her blouse, betraying her anxiety.

Mr. Miller's wife quickly glanced at Mr. Miller, then back at Ioanna's retreating figure, as if assessing the situation. Kai observed these details with a professional's eye, noting the way her behavior contrasted sharply with the polite façade she had maintained earlier. Her unease seemed genuine, and Kai mentally cataloged her reaction, intrigued by the subtle tension that had surfaced.

The moment Ioanna was out of sight, Mr. Miller's wife turned her attention back to Kai, her expression now carefully composed but with a lingering hint of wariness. Kai's observations of the subtle changes in her demeanor further fueled his curiosity about the hotel and its occupants, adding another layer to his growing suspicion of the hotel's enigmatic atmosphere.

Kai, maintaining his calm and professional demeanor, turned to Mr. Miller and asked, "Are there any good locations to visit nearby? We're looking for some recommendations."

Mr. Miller's face lit up with enthusiasm again, but it was clear he was straining to offer a suggestion. "Well," he said, "there are many beautiful spots around Manali. If you're interested in scenic views, I'd recommend visiting the Solang Valley. It's renowned for its breathtaking landscapes and adventure activities. Also, you might enjoy the Rohtang Pass, though it's a bit further out. It offers spectacular mountain views."

Kai nodded appreciatively. "Thank you for the suggestion. It sounds like a wonderful place to explore."

Mr. Miller then extended a friendly offer. "If you're free, Mr. Starling, and feel comfortable, why don't you join us for a visit to Solang Valley tomorrow morning? It could be a great opportunity to explore the area together."

Kai considered the invitation briefly before responding with a polite smile. "I appreciate the offer, Mr. Miller, but I have some personal work to attend to. I'm sure Solang Valley will be amazing. Thank you for your kind invitation, and I'll keep it in mind."

With a final nod, Kai excused himself. As he walked away, he took one last look around the lobby, his mind still churning with observations and suspicions about the people and the atmosphere of the hotel. The interaction with Mr. Miller had provided new insights, but Kai's curiosity about the underlying tensions remained piqued.

The next morning, Kai was roused from his sleep by a series of knocks on the door. Knock, knock! He turned to see Ioanna still deeply asleep beside him. Not wanting to disturb her, he got up and went to the door. When he opened it, he was greeted by Mr. Miller, who was standing there with a cheerful smile. "Good morning, Mr. Starling," he said. "I hope you haven't forgotten about our visit to Solang Valley! I've prepared everything for the trip. Why don't you get ready, and we can have breakfast together before we head out?"

Kai nodded, a bit surprised but intrigued by Mr. Miller's enthusiasm. "Sure, I'll just wake up Ioanna and be ready shortly."

As he closed the door, he felt a mix of anticipation and curiosity about the day ahead.

Kai walked back to the bed, where Ioanna was now sitting up, rubbing her eyes. "Okay, Ioanna! Oh, you're already awake!" he said, a bit surprised.

Ioanna chuckled softly. "Why not? If someone's knocking at the door this early in the morning, I figured I might as well get up!"

Kai smiled, appreciating her good humor. "Alright then, get ready. We need to head out soon. Mr. Miller's arranged everything for our trip to Solang Valley."

Ioanna nodded and started getting ready, her excitement about the day ahead evident. Kai, too, prepared for the adventure, looking forward to the day's exploration and hoping to uncover more about the mysterious circumstances of their stay.

After enjoying breakfast with Mr. Miller and his wife, Kai listened intently as Mr. Miller shared an intriguing piece of local news. "You know," Mr. Miller began, taking a big bite of his jam toast, "a few days ago, there was a serious accident here in the mountains. A person was caught by a sliding rock while hiking and ended up in very bad condition."

Kai's interest was piqued. "That sounds terrible. Do they know how it happened?"

Mr. Miller nodded, his expression serious. "Yes, it was quite a scare. The rescue teams managed to get the person to the hospital, but they're still in critical condition. It's been quite the talk around here."

As Kai absorbed this new information, he couldn't help but wonder if this incident might somehow connect to the other tensions he had noticed.

After finishing breakfast, Kai, Ioanna, and Mr. Miller, along with his wife, were ready to head to Solang Valley. They stepped outside to find their car waiting in front of the hotel. As they drove off, the journey unfolded with breathtaking scenery. The road wound through lush green valleys, towering pine trees, and rugged mountain peaks, each turn revealing a more stunning view than the last. The early morning light cast a golden hue over the landscape, highlighting the vibrant colors of blooming wildflowers and the sparkling streams that meandered alongside the road.

As they approached Solang Valley, the beauty of the place was even more spectacular. The valley was a picturesque expanse of verdant meadows surrounded by snow-capped peaks, with the Beas River flowing gently through the landscape. The air was crisp and invigorating, filled with the sounds of chirping birds and the distant rush of the river. The valley was dotted with colorful tents and bustling activity, as tourists and locals alike enjoyed the day.

Ioanna's face lit up with happiness as she took in the scene. Kai and Ioanna posed for pictures against the backdrop of the magnificent valley, capturing the moments of joy and wonder.

At one point, Mr. Miller, ever the entertainer, came over with a large, playful smile. His wife, in a moment of affectionate humor, gently grabbed his ears, eliciting laughter from everyone around. The lightheartedness and camaraderie of the group added to the warmth of the day.

After a day filled with laughter, exploration, and the sheer beauty of Solang Valley, they headed back to the hotel, their hearts full of cherished memories from a perfect day.

The group returned to the hotel after their delightful trip to Solang Valley, the peaceful atmosphere of the day began to shift. The evening had set in, casting long shadows over the hotel, and a strange tension filled the air.

While walking through the lobby, Kai noticed an unusual commotion near the front desk. A few guests were whispering anxiously, and the hotel staff seemed on edge. Sensing something was wrong, Kai exchanged a glance with Ioanna, who immediately caught on to his unease.

Just then, Mr. Miller hurried over, his usual jovial expression replaced by one of concern. "I don't mean to alarm you," he said quietly, "but there's been an incident. A guest was found... unconscious in their room. It seems there's more to it than just an accident."

Kai's instincts kicked in immediately. He had sensed something was off earlier, and now it was clear that something sinister was at play. "What happened exactly?" Kai asked, his voice steady but intense.

Mr. Miller glanced around, lowering his voice even further. "The guest was a man staying on the same floor as us. Room 302. The staff found him with head trauma, but there are no signs of a break-in. It looks... deliberate, but no one knows how it happened."

Kai's mind raced. No break-in? No witnesses? This wasn't a random accident—it was too clean, too calculated.

He turned to Ioanna, his expression serious. "Go back to our room. Stay safe, and don't leave until I return."

Ioanna nodded, her eyes filled with worry, but she trusted Kai's instincts. As she hurried toward their room, Kai made his way to the third floor, where the crime scene was. His mind raced with questions, his instincts sharp and ready.

The hallway was eerily quiet, the door to Room 302 slightly ajar. He approached cautiously, the silence unsettling. Pushing the door open, Kai stepped inside. The air was cold, unnaturally so, and something felt off, like the room itself held its breath.

The sight before him made his skin crawl. The victim lay on the floor, a man in his forties, his body twisted unnaturally, as if he'd fought his attacker. No sign of forced entry. No obvious weapon. Just a deep gash on the side of his head, as if something blunt had struck him.

Kai's eyes narrowed. This wasn't an accident. The placement of the body, the pristine condition of the rest of the room—it was staged, but to what end? He crouched down, scanning the floor for clues. His fingers grazed something under the bed, a small piece of paper folded tightly.

He opened it slowly. A name was scribbled hastily—Ioanna.

His heart skipped a beat. Was she the next target?

Suddenly, the door creaked behind him. Kai whipped around to see a shadow retreating down the hall. Someone had been watching him. Without hesitation, he darted out of the room, racing down the hall, but whoever it was had already vanished.

Kai's mind raced. Someone was after them. But who? And why?

His breath quickened as he hurried back to their room. Bursting through the door, he found Ioanna sitting on the bed, startled by his sudden entrance. "Kai, what's going on?"

"We're not safe here," he said, his voice low but urgent. "Someone's targeting us. I found your name at the scene."

Ioanna's face paled. "What do you mean?"

Before Kai could answer, a loud knock came from the door. They both froze. Kai signaled for her to stay quiet as he slowly approached, peeking through the peephole.

It was Mr. Miller.

"Good evening, Mr. Starling," he said, his voice calm but somehow ominous. "I hope I'm not disturbing you. Just wanted to see if you and your wife were ready for the next part of the adventure."

Kai felt a chill run down his spine. Something wasn't right.

Kai hesitated before opening the door, his instincts telling him to stay on guard. Mr. Miller stood there with his signature smile, but Kai could see something different this time. A flicker of unease, something darker behind the man's friendly demeanor.

"Mr. Starling, are you all set for our next excursion?" Mr. Miller asked, his voice smooth but somehow off-putting.

Kai forced a polite smile, stepping into the hallway and closing the door gently behind him to keep Ioanna out of earshot. "Actually, I'm not sure if we'll make it tonight. Something's come up." He watched Mr. Miller closely, gauging his reaction.

"Is that so?" Miller's smile faltered for just a moment, and Kai caught the brief tension in his jaw. "A shame. I was really looking forward to showing you both more of the valley."

Kai nodded, his mind piecing together fragments of the puzzle. Something about Mr. Miller's timing was too perfect, his presence at key moments unsettling. And the fact that the note found at the crime scene had Ioanna's name on it—that couldn't be a coincidence.

As Kai excused himself, he watched Mr. Miller walk away, whistling softly under his breath. Kai's mind was racing, the pieces starting to fit together, but there was still something missing—something just out of reach.

Back inside the room, Kai sat down next to Ioanna, his face tense with concentration.

"What's wrong, Kai? What did Mr. Miller want?" Ioanna asked, worry clear in her voice.

He sighed and leaned in closer. "I think Miller is connected to what's happening. The timing of everything... it's too perfect. And I found something at the crime scene—a note with your name on it. Whoever is behind this knows we're here, and they're trying to get into our heads."

Ioanna's eyes widened. "What do we do now?"

Kai's mind was already working, sorting through the clues. The murder in Room 302, the note with Ioanna's name, Miller's strange behavior—there had to be a connection.

"First, we need to figure out what Miller's role in all this is," Kai said. "He's playing a game, but we don't know the rules yet. We'll keep up the act, pretend we don't suspect anything, but I need to gather more information."

As Kai stood up, something caught his eye—a small, barely noticeable smudge of dirt near the doorframe. It was out of place, too precise to be an accident. Bending down, he ran his fingers over it, feeling a cold shiver run down his spine. It was recent, as if someone had been here, watching.

He straightened up, his voice low. "We're being watched, Ioanna. Someone was just outside this room."

Ioanna gasped, her eyes darting toward the door. "What do we do?"

Kai's jaw tightened. "We act like nothing's wrong. I'm going to do some digging, but we need to be careful. Whatever this is, it's dangerous—and they're targeting you for a reason."

As the evening wore on, Kai couldn't shake the feeling that the entire hotel was part of a larger game. The more he thought about it, the more certain he became that the murder in Room 302 wasn't random. It was a message. And Miller, with his over-friendly nature and impeccable timing, was part of the puzzle.

Kai slipped out of their room later that night, determined to gather more clues. He headed to the hotel's front desk, hoping to find something useful. As he scanned the guestbook, his eyes stopped on an entry that made his blood run cold.

Room 302 was registered to someone under the name of "Mr. Starling."

His own name.

Suddenly, it all made sense. Someone was trying to frame him, to pull him into a twisted game. And Ioanna was being used as bait.

Just as Kai's mind raced through the possibilities, a knock on the door startled both him and Ioanna. His instincts sharpened, he reached for the door slowly, the weight of the tension thick in the air.

Outside, two police officers stood waiting, their expressions stern but curious. One of them, a tall woman with piercing blue eyes and an authoritative stance, stepped forward.

"Mr. Starling, I presume?" she said, her voice sharp, professional. "I'm Officer Neha Verma. We're here to ask you and your wife some questions."

Kai noticed her eyes dart toward Ioanna, quickly assessing her, before shifting back to him. He nodded, letting them into the room.

"Is something wrong?" Ioanna asked, her voice nervous but steady.

Officer Verma's partner, a stocky man with a trimmed beard, spoke up. "We've been investigating the incident in Room 302, and we found some… troubling evidence." He pulled out a small notebook, flipping through the pages. "Your name, Mr. Starling, came up in our records. Seems like you're connected to the person who stayed in that room."

Kai felt a chill crawl up his spine. He knew it wasn't a coincidence.

"Connected?" Kai asked, his tone calm though his mind was racing. "I don't even know the person staying there."

"Are you sure about that?" Officer Verma asked, her eyes narrowing. "The name listed on the guest registration for Room 302 is also 'Mr. Starling.' Same initials. Same name. Different person? Or something else?"

Kai clenched his jaw, the gears in his mind turning rapidly. It was too calculated—someone was trying to frame him, but why?

"It's a common name," Kai replied evenly, "but I assure you, Officer, I have nothing to do with this. I'm a private investigator. My wife and I are here for a vacation, nothing more."

Verma's gaze hardened as if weighing the truth in his words. She was sharp, no doubt about it, but Kai knew she wasn't the mastermind behind this puzzle. She was just a piece in it.

"We'll need you both to stay in the hotel while we continue the investigation," she said, handing them her card. "And if you think of anything—anything at all that might help, call us."

The officers left, but the tension remained, thickening the air around them. Kai knew that time was running out. The police were starting to suspect him, and whoever was behind the framing was closing in fast.

After a few moments of silence, Ioanna whispered, "Kai… what do we do?"

He stood still for a moment, his brain calculating every detail. "We don't have much time, Ioanna. Whoever is behind this wants us to panic. But we won't. We're going to stay one step ahead."

Kai pulled out his phone and began scrolling through old contacts. He dialed a number—one he hadn't used in years. After a few rings, a gruff voice answered.

"Detective Mukherjee," Kai said quietly. "It's Kai. I need your help."

Meanwhile, Ioanna paced nervously, her eyes darting toward the door as though she expected someone to burst in any second. The eerie stillness of the hotel only added to her unease.

"Who are you calling?" she asked.

"An old friend in the force. We need backup, someone on our side who can help us sort through this mess without falling into whoever's trap this is." He paused and looked at her. "Ioanna, I need you to trust me."

Before Ioanna could respond, the power in the room flickered, casting the room into brief darkness. When the lights came back on, a cold draft swept through the room. It wasn't just the hotel playing tricks—it was something more sinister.

Kai's eyes darted to the small balcony. The sliding glass door was slightly ajar.

Ioanna gasped, pointing toward the corner of the room. On the floor, under the curtain, lay a small envelope—a piece of parchment with his name written in bold, sharp handwriting.

Kai grabbed it and tore it open, revealing a single, chilling line:

"Solve the puzzle, or she dies."

His heart raced, adrenaline pumping through his veins. Someone had been inside the room. They were toying with him, pushing him to solve this twisted game, but the stakes had just been raised. It was no longer just about him—it was Ioanna's life on the line now.

Kai's mind buzzed with every clue, every conversation, every hidden message. Mr.

Miller's strange behavior, the timing of the murder, and now this—the threat was clear, but the motives were murky.

"We need to go," Kai muttered, gathering his things. "It's not safe here."

Just as he said it, another knock came at the door.

"Mr. Starling! Open up, it's Miller!" came a voice from outside. It was cheerful, but Kai could hear the urgency beneath it. He hesitated for a moment before answering, but kept Ioanna close behind him.

Miller stood there, grinning, but his eyes betrayed a flicker of something darker. "Hope I'm not interrupting. Thought I'd check in on you two after all that excitement."

Kai studied him. Miller's facade was starting to crack. He was hiding something, and Kai needed to figure out what before it was too late.

"Miller," Kai said, forcing a smile. "Actually, there's something I've been meaning to ask you…"

But before he could finish, the power went out again. This time, it didn't come back on.

Ioanna let out a small scream as the room plunged into darkness. Kai pulled her close, his hand instinctively reaching for the small knife he kept in his jacket.

"Miller?" he called out into the darkness, but there was no response.

Instead, a chilling voice echoed from the hallway. "Tick tock, Mr. Starling... time is running out."

Kai's mind whirred, piecing together every subtle clue from the last few days. The warning in the letter, the flickering power, and the strange timing of Miller's sudden appearance—everything was part of a much bigger plot. But how big? And why Ioanna?

As the darkness surrounded them, Ioanna's breathing became erratic. She tugged on Kai's sleeve, whispering, "Kai... that voice... it sounded familiar."

He squeezed her hand, a sense of dread settling over him. "Familiar how?"

"I... I heard it before," Ioanna said, her voice trembling. "On the flight... the day I had that nightmare about losing you."

Kai's mind flashed back to the flight—Ioanna had woken up, drenched in fear, her words scrambled as she muttered about seeing Kai die. Back then, he had brushed it off as just a bad dream. But now, in the midst of all this, something clicked.

That wasn't just a dream. It was a setup.

"Stay here," Kai whispered to Ioanna, his voice firm yet calm. He grabbed his phone and turned on the flashlight feature. The faint beam cut through the darkness, giving them a small sense of safety. But it wasn't enough.

His mind raced back to the flight. There had been a man sitting behind them, one Kai had caught glancing at Ioanna a few too many times. He remembered the uneasy feeling that had gnawed at him during the journey but had brushed it off as travel anxiety. What if that man had been part of this the whole time?

Suddenly, a muffled noise came from the hallway. Kai instinctively moved closer to Ioanna, his body tense.

"Miller!" Kai barked into the blackness, but there was no response. The only sound was the soft hum of the wind outside and the pounding of his heart. He had to act fast.

"Ioanna, you remember the driver who picked us up at Bhuntar airport?" he asked suddenly.

She nodded, confused. "Yes, but why?"

Kai's eyes darkened with realization. "He was acting strange. Too eager to get us here. And I remember now... he avoided eye contact when I asked him about his name. It wasn't just him, though. The flight attendant who gave you that drink before you fell asleep—she was involved too."

Ioanna's face turned pale. "Are you saying that… they drugged me?"

"Exactly," Kai said, piecing it together. "That dream you had on the flight—it wasn't a dream. Someone drugged you with hallucinogens, and they planted that image in your mind. They wanted you to think I died so you'd be shaken, vulnerable."

Before they could process the gravity of it all, another knock came at the door, this one more frantic. Kai swung it open cautiously, his heart pounding.

Standing there was the driver from Bhuntar Airport—his eyes wild, his breathing heavy.

"Kai, sir... you have to listen to me," the driver stammered, his voice shaking. "I—I had no choice. They made me do it. They're watching us all."

Kai narrowed his eyes, pulling the driver into the room and closing the door. "What are you talking about? Who made you do what?"

The driver glanced nervously around the room as if expecting someone to jump out of the shadows. "The man on the flight... the one sitting behind you. He's not alone. There's a group—something bigger than you think. They've been following you since you landed. I—I was just supposed to keep an eye on you, report back to them... but now it's out of control."

Kai's hand tightened around the small knife he kept in his pocket. "Who are they? What do they want?"

Before the driver could answer, there was a sudden loud crash from the hallway, followed by a chilling scream. Ioanna gasped, and Kai rushed to the door again, pulling it open to find Miller lying in the hallway, blood pooling beneath him.

"Oh my god!" Ioanna cried, clutching Kai's arm.

Kai knelt beside Miller, his pulse pounding in his ears. Miller was still alive but barely. His eyes flickered open, and he rasped out a few broken words. "You… have to… stop them… it's all connected…"

With that, Miller's eyes rolled back, and his body went limp.

The driver was shaking now, his face pale. "They're coming for all of us! You have to trust me, I had no choice."

Kai stood up, pulling Ioanna close. "We need to get out of here. Now."

Just as he turned to grab their things, the door at the end of the hall creaked open, and the silhouette of a man stepped into the dim light. His face was obscured, but there was no mistaking the chilling presence he carried with him.

It was the man from the flight.

He slowly walked toward them, his footsteps eerily calm, as though he had all the time in the world. Kai's instincts kicked in, every muscle in his body ready for action.

But before he could move, the man spoke.

"Mr. Starling," the man said, his voice cold and calculating. "You've done well to survive this long. But the game is far from over."

Kai felt the hairs on the back of his neck stand up. "What do you want?"

The man smiled, a cruel twist of his lips. "I want you to finish what you started. Solve the puzzle, or lose everything."

The driver suddenly bolted, running down the hall, but a shot rang out, and he collapsed, the echo of the gunfire ringing in the narrow corridor.

Ioanna screamed, and Kai yanked her back into the room, slamming the door shut. He leaned against it, breathing hard, his mind racing for answers.

There was no more time. No more guessing. This had become more than just a vacation gone wrong—this was a game, and they were all pawns.

"They've been playing us from the start," Kai said under his breath. "The flight, the hotel, Miller... even the dream you had, Ioanna—it was all planned. And now, they're tightening the noose."

Ioanna's voice quivered as she spoke, "Kai, how do we get out of this?"

Kai's eyes hardened. He knew what needed to be done. "We outsmart them. We play their game, but on our terms. They want me to solve the puzzle? Fine. But I'm not going to let them hurt you."

He turned to Ioanna, his hand reaching for hers, steady and strong. "We're going to figure this out, piece by piece. But first, we need to make sure we're not alone. I need to contact someone who can help."

Kai's mind raced as he pulled Ioanna closer, every instinct on high alert. The mysterious man from the flight stood there, his presence exuding a chilling calmness that only heightened the danger.

"We need to get out of here," Kai whispered, his eyes scanning the room for an escape route. But his gaze was drawn back to the man, who seemed to relish the chaos he'd created.

The man's smile widened. "You're clever, Mr. Starling. But do you really think you can solve this puzzle before it's too late?"

Kai's eyes narrowed. "I don't play games with lives. What's the real motive behind all this?"

The man's expression darkened. "It's not about the motive. It's about control. And you're the key to it all."

Kai felt a sudden, uncomfortable shift in the air, as though something significant was about to be revealed. "Control? What do you mean?"

The man's lips curled into a cruel grin. "The real game began on that flight. The dream Ioanna had was engineered to destabilize you both. The driver, the flight attendant—everyone was a pawn. But you, Kai Starling, you're the centerpiece."

As the man spoke, Kai's mind raced through every clue. The driver, the flight attendant, the strange coincidences—they were all linked to one central figure, manipulating everything from the shadows.

Kai's gaze hardened. "And you're the mastermind behind it all."

The man's grin widened. "Precisely. I've orchestrated this entire scenario to test your skills, to see if you can unravel the web I've spun. The stakes are high, and the game is far from over."

Suddenly, Kai's phone buzzed with a new message. It was from an unknown number. He opened it to find a video clip—an image of the man from the flight meeting with several high-profile figures in a clandestine meeting. The footage revealed their plan to undermine global security through a series of coordinated attacks.

The realization hit Kai like a thunderbolt. "You're not just playing a game. You're part of a global conspiracy."

The man's eyes gleamed with dark satisfaction. "Correct. And you're going to help us bring it to fruition—or else."

Kai's mind worked furiously. He had to act fast. He turned to Ioanna. "Stay here, and keep low. I need to confront this man and stop him before it's too late."

With a steely resolve, Kai approached the man, his demeanor shifting from calculated calm to intense focus. "You think you've outsmarted me? Think again."

Kai moved swiftly, disarming the man with precise, fluid motions. He used his skills in hand-to-hand combat, honed from years of experience, to incapacitate him without causing unnecessary harm.

As the man struggled, Kai pulled out a hidden earpiece and activated it, contacting his trusted allies who had been tracking the conspiracy from a distance.

"This is Kai Starling," he said into the earpiece. "I've uncovered the full extent of the plot. We need immediate backup and extraction."

Within moments, a team of operatives burst into the room, neutralizing the remaining threats and securing the area. Kai's allies took the man into custody, ensuring that he would face justice for his actions.

Ioanna watched in awe as Kai, with a mixture of relief and determination, approached her. "It's over," he said. "For now. But there's more work to be done."

As they left the hotel, Kai glanced back, his mind already focused on the next steps. The puzzle was solved, but the consequences of the conspiracy would ripple far beyond this single event.

Ioanna, still processing the gravity of it all, looked at Kai with newfound respect and admiration. "How did you know?"

Kai's gaze was steady. "It's not about knowing. It's about seeing the pieces of the puzzle and putting them together before it's too late."

As they walked away, the night air was filled with a sense of resolution. Kai had faced the ultimate challenge and emerged victorious, but the road ahead promised more trials and revelations.

As they emerged from the hotel, Kai and Ioanna were greeted by the cool, crisp night air. The oppressive weight of the conspiracy had lifted slightly, but the danger was far from over. Kai's mind was already on high alert, analyzing every detail and preparing for the next move.

They reached a secluded area, away from the chaos of the hotel. Ioanna looked at Kai, her eyes filled with a mix of awe and concern. "What's the plan now?"

Kai's gaze was intense, his demeanor calm but resolute. "We need to make sure we're safe and find out who else is involved in this conspiracy. But first, I need to show you something."

Without warning, Kai pulled out a small, inconspicuous device from his pocket and placed it on the ground. He pressed a button, and a holographic interface flickered to life, projecting a detailed map of the area.

Ioanna's eyes widened as Kai navigated through the map with swift, precise movements. "This is an advanced surveillance system," he explained. "I've been tracking their movements and monitoring their communications for weeks."

He tapped a few more commands, and the hologram shifted to reveal real-time footage of several locations across the city. Kai pointed to a specific spot. "This is where their next operation is planned. We need to get there before they can execute their plans."

Before Ioanna could respond, Kai's phone buzzed with an incoming call. He answered with a curt, professional tone. "Starling here."

The voice on the other end was panicked. "Kai, we've detected a significant increase in their activity. They're preparing for a large-scale attack. You need to act quickly."

Kai's expression hardened. "Understood. I'll handle it."

He ended the call and turned to Ioanna. "This isn't just about solving puzzles anymore. This is about stopping a global threat."

Without another word, Kai took off at a rapid pace, his movements fluid and precise. Ioanna struggled to keep up, but Kai's focus was unwavering. They navigated through the city with a combination of speed and stealth, avoiding surveillance and outmaneuvering any potential threats.

As they approached the designated location, Kai's senses were heightened. He slipped into the building with a practiced ease, moving silently through the shadows. Ioanna followed closely, her heart pounding in her chest.

Inside, Kai's eyes scanned the room, noting every detail—the placement of security cameras, the positioning of guards, and the layout of the facility. He used his skills in close combat to neutralize the guards swiftly and silently, his movements a blur of efficiency.

When they reached the central control room, Kai's fingers flew over the keyboard, hacking into the system with astonishing speed. The screens in the room flickered as he dismantled the planned attack, overriding their protocols and ensuring that their operation was neutralized.

The mastermind behind the conspiracy, the man from the flight, watched through hidden cameras, his face contorted in frustration. "How is this possible? How did he get here so quickly?"

Kai's voice crackled through the intercom, calm and authoritative. "Your plans have been foiled. Your web of deceit ends here."

With the control room secured and the attack thwarted, Kai and Ioanna made their way out, their path clear. The sense of urgency had faded, replaced by a profound sense of accomplishment.

Ioanna looked at Kai with a mix of admiration and awe. "How did you do all that?"

Kai's gaze was steady, a faint smile playing at the corners of his lips. "Years of training and experience. But it's not just about skills. It's about understanding the enemy and staying one step ahead."

As they walked away from the scene, the weight of the night's events began to settle in. The danger had passed, but the road ahead was still fraught with challenges. Kai's resolve remained unshaken, his determination to protect and serve stronger than ever.

As Kai and Ioanna left the facility, the reality of their victory settled in. They had a moment of respite, but Kai knew the final puzzle pieces needed to be put in place to fully understand the conspiracy and its terrifying scope.

They reached a safehouse, where Kai set up a makeshift command center. He connected his device to the facility's mainframe and began sifting through the data. Ioanna watched, her nerves frayed but her curiosity piqued.

"What are you looking for?" she asked, her voice trembling.

Kai didn't look up from the screen. "I need to understand who orchestrated this, why, and how deep the conspiracy runs."

As he worked, images and documents began to reveal a chilling narrative. The footage and files he accessed detailed the conspiracy's origins—a shadowy organization that had been manipulating events from behind the scenes, causing chaos and instability across the globe.

Kai's eyes were steely as he pieced together the information. "This organization, known as 'The Nexus,' has been behind numerous global incidents. They thrive on chaos and use it to control governments and corporations."

Ioanna's face paled. "And the people involved—the driver, the flight attendant..."

Kai nodded grimly. "They were all operatives, but their roles were much deeper than we realized. The driver's task was to monitor us, ensuring we were where they wanted us. The flight attendant was involved in drugging you to destabilize me. Everything was calculated to keep us off balance and control the outcome."

The final piece of the puzzle was a hidden message embedded in the facility's security system. Kai decoded it, revealing the mastermind's identity: a powerful and influential figure who had used their position to orchestrate the entire conspiracy. The message also detailed their ultimate goal: to execute a massive coordinated attack to plunge the world into chaos, creating a power vacuum they could exploit.

Kai's face hardened. "They planned to strike during the most vulnerable moment, using the chaos to seize control. Their plan was nearly flawless, but we exposed it just in time."

Ioanna's hands shook as she took in the magnitude of their near-catastrophe. "How could they be so ruthless?"

Kai's expression was grim. "They're driven by power and control. They thrive on fear and manipulate events to their advantage. But we stopped them. They won't get a chance to execute their plans."

Kai's phone buzzed with a call from his allies. "The Nexus has been apprehended. We've secured the key players, and their plans have been dismantled."

As the news sank in, a sense of relief washed over them. But the terror of what might have happened lingered. Kai turned to Ioanna, his eyes softening.

"We faced something truly terrifying, but we made it through," he said. "You were incredibly brave."

Ioanna's voice was filled with a mix of exhaustion and relief. "I couldn't have done it without you."

Kai's gaze was resolute. "It's not over. There will always be threats, but as long as we stay vigilant, we can protect the world from the shadows."

As they left the safehouse, the dawn began to break, casting a new light on their journey. The nightmare had been averted, but the scars of their ordeal would remain as a reminder of the darkness they had faced and the strength they had found within themselves.

Together, they stepped into the morning light, ready to embrace whatever came next with courage and determination.

The first light of dawn touched the horizon, Kai and Ioanna stood outside, taking in the serenity that followed their harrowing night. The city lay calm, unaware of the catastrophe that had been narrowly avoided.

Kai's phone buzzed with final updates from his team. The remaining members of The Nexus had been apprehended, their intricate network dismantled. The global threat had been neutralized, and the world was safe once more.

Ioanna turned to Kai, her expression a blend of relief and reflection. "What happens now?"

Kai took her hand, a reassuring smile on his face. "We move forward. We rebuild and heal from the scars of this experience. But we also remember the strength we discovered in ourselves and each other."

They decided to take a few days to recuperate, staying at a quiet retreat in the hills of Manali, away from the chaos. As they walked through the lush greenery, they reflected on their journey. The darkness they had faced had been daunting, but it had forged a bond between them that was unbreakable.

Kai's mind was already turning to the future. He knew that the fight against hidden threats was ongoing, but he felt ready for whatever came next. His skills and resolve had been tested, and he emerged stronger, more determined, and deeply connected to Ioanna.

Ioanna, too, felt a newfound sense of purpose. The ordeal had been terrifying, but it had also shown her the depth of Kai's courage and the power of their partnership. She knew they would face any challenge together, drawing strength from their shared experiences.

As they stood on a hill overlooking the valley, the sun casting its golden glow over the landscape, they embraced the promise of a new beginning. The shadows of their past would always be a part of them, but they were no longer defined by them. They had triumphed over fear, found clarity in chaos, and emerged into the light with renewed hope.

Together, they looked out at the world, ready to embrace the future with a sense of purpose and a heart full of resilience.

Chapter 3

The First Shot

The early morning fog clung to the ground as Ioanna stood at the window, her mind still clouded with the terrifying events of the past few days. She needed to feel Kai's presence, to honor the man who had once stood by her side, always vigilant and ready. But there was something more—a mystery still lingering, pulling her deeper into his past.

As she sipped her tea, she noticed an envelope on the table, left unopened since the night before. Her hands trembled as she recognized the seal: it was from Kai's old crime division. He rarely spoke about his work, but now she needed answers. With a deep breath, she opened the letter.

It was an old case file.

The First Crime He Solved.

Years ago, Kai had been an ordinary software engineer. He was quiet but observant, always noticing things others missed. His sharp mind was not limited to computers; it worked through problems like a detective solving a puzzle. And it was during a routine project at a corporate office in Kolkata when he first encountered the kind of situation that would change the course of his life.

The CEO of the company, an influential man named Amitabh Roy, had been murdered in his office. The police were baffled—no signs of forced entry, no witnesses, and the surveillance cameras had mysteriously malfunctioned during the time of the crime.

Kai had no official reason to be involved in the investigation. But something didn't sit right with him. The way people in the office reacted, the little clues they left behind, the strange way Roy's assistant spoke—it gnawed at him.

He remembered walking into that office after hours, his curiosity driving him to retrace the last known steps of the victim. And that's when he saw it—the smallest, most insignificant detail that the police had overlooked.

A misplaced pen.

It wasn't the pen itself but where it was located—far from the desk, near the bookshelf. Kai's mind began piecing things together. He remembered the layout of the office and how it didn't make sense for the pen to be there unless someone had been in a struggle. And that's when he noticed something else: the bookshelf was slightly ajar.

With the precision of a man born for this work, Kai discovered a hidden compartment behind the shelf. Inside were files that implicated Roy in a massive corporate scandal, evidence that would have ruined his reputation. But that wasn't all.

The next clue had been in Roy's hand. A tiny slip of paper with a single name: Suresh.

It didn't take long for Kai to connect the dots. Suresh, Roy's long-time associate and someone who had everything to gain from Roy's death, had orchestrated the murder. He had access to the office, knew the camera system, and had even planted false evidence to frame an innocent employee.

But Kai had figured it out, and with that, he presented the evidence to the police, clearing the employee's name and setting Suresh on the path to justice. The case had earned him quiet recognition, and soon after, Kai was recruited into a private investigative unit.

As Ioanna read through the file, her heart swelled with pride. This was Kai at his core—a man who couldn't ignore the truth even if it put him in harm's way. She knew then that his investigation into their current situation had followed the same relentless pattern. He had always been a step ahead, and she couldn't afford to fall behind.

Suddenly, a sharp knock at the door broke her thoughts. She froze, remembering the warning from the night before. Her eyes darted to the door, and her pulse quickened.

"Who is it?" she asked, her voice steadier than she felt.

No answer.

She moved closer to the door, her heart pounding louder with every step. When she reached for the handle, the door flew open, and there stood a man—a face she recognized from the hotel.

It was the driver. But this time, he wasn't alone.

Kai crouched behind a pile of crates in the alleyway, his gun drawn, his mind sharp and focused. The air was thick with tension as he watched the silhouettes moving against the dim streetlights. He had anticipated this, knowing that their enemies would come for them the moment they realized he was still alive and fighting back.

He wasn't just a detective anymore; this was personal.

As he gripped the gun, memories of his first case flooded back—the adrenaline, the clarity of each moment, and the danger that came with it. He had been prepared to shoot that day too, but it hadn't come to that. This time, it would.

His phone buzzed. Ioanna's name flashed on the screen.

"Kai, they're here," she whispered, fear evident in her voice.

"I'm on my way," he said, his voice calm but lethal. "Stay low."

He cut the call and moved swiftly, his gun ready. He had trained for this, and no one was going to harm Ioanna. Not again.

The door burst open, and Ioanna stumbled backward, her mind racing. She had no weapon, no way to defend herself, but she had something else—faith in Kai. He would come. He always did.

The driver stepped forward, his face twisted with fear. "I told you—this is bigger than you think. They'll kill me if I don't follow through."

"Who are they?" Ioanna demanded, her voice shaking. "What do they want?"

Before the driver could answer, a shot rang out. The driver collapsed to the ground, a bullet hole in his chest, and Ioanna screamed.

Kai stood in the doorway, his gun smoking, his eyes cold and calculating. He had seen enough to know that hesitation would only get them killed.

"Get up," he said, his voice commanding but gentle. "We're leaving."

Ioanna ran to him, her heart still racing from the gunshot, but she knew better than to question him. He pulled her close, checking the hallway for any more threats.

"Whoever's behind this is trying to cover their tracks," Kai said as they moved quickly through the building. "But I know who's pulling the strings now. It's not over yet, Ioanna."

His voice was steady, but Ioanna could feel the tension in the air. They were in deeper than she had realized, and the real threat was still out there.

As they stepped outside into the cold night, Ioanna looked at him, her heart swelling with admiration. This was Kai—the man who had solved his first crime with a sharp mind and quiet resolve. And now, he was using those same skills to protect her, to unravel the most terrifying mystery of their lives.

But the question still lingered: Who was behind this? And why had they targeted Ioanna?

The Thunderstorm of Shadows

As the storm outside raged, lightning flashed across the night sky, casting eerie shadows on the walls of the remote safehouse where Kai and Ioanna found themselves. They had escaped the hotel, but danger still loomed, unseen but felt in every flicker of the storm.

The winds howled outside, but inside, there was an eerie silence as Kai paced, his mind piecing together the puzzle that had been unraveling since the murder in the hotel. His gun rested on the table beside him, within arm's reach, and his eyes were sharp, scanning every corner of the room. Ioanna sat on the couch, clutching a blanket, her nerves still rattled from the events of the night.

Suddenly, the door creaked open, and Kai's instincts kicked in. He grabbed his gun and aimed at the shadow that appeared in the doorway.

"Whoa! It's me!"

The voice was familiar—too familiar. Kai lowered his gun with a sigh of relief, a small smile tugging at his lips.

"Rehaan."

Rehaan Kapoor stepped into the room, his face hardened by years of experience but softened by the sight of his old friend. He was Kai's former partner in the investigative unit, a man who had seen it all. Together, they had solved some of the toughest cases, but a falling out years ago had led them down separate paths. Now, Rehaan was back.

Rehaan, taller and broader than Kai, carried an air of confidence. His sharp eyes scanned the room as if assessing every potential threat. He tossed his rain-soaked jacket on a chair and grinned.

"You still have that killer instinct, Kai," he said, shaking his head. "Nice to see you haven't lost it."

Kai nodded, but the tension in the air was thick. Their reunion was welcome, but the circumstances were dire.

"I had no choice but to call you," Kai said, his voice heavy. "Things are getting out of hand. We're dealing with something big. It's all connected to the murder in the hotel."

Rehaan's expression darkened as he walked toward the table, his eyes narrowing as he took in the scattered evidence Kai had laid out.

"From what you told me, this goes way beyond just a simple murder. Whoever's pulling the strings—" Rehaan paused, glancing at Ioanna, who looked lost in thought. "—they're dangerous. Ruthless. We're up against something bigger than either of us ever anticipated."

Miles away, in the heart of the city, a sleek, dark car pulled up to a secluded mansion. Inside, the true puppet master of the deadly game was ready to make her next move.

In the dim light of her luxurious office, Meera Khanna—a name feared in the underworld and respected by the elites—stood by the window, watching the storm with a smile. Her carefully crafted web of power and corruption had ensnared countless souls, and now Kai had walked right into her trap.

Her assistant, a tall man named Vikram, entered quietly, holding a tablet with the latest updates.

"Madam, Kai and Ioanna have escaped the hotel, but Rehaan has joined them," Vikram said, his voice steady.

Meera's eyes gleamed with dark excitement. She had orchestrated every move, and now the real game was about to begin.

"Good," she said, her voice low and filled with malice. "Let them think they're winning. I have everything in place. When the time is right, we'll make our final move. But for now... let them suffer in the storm."

She turned, her expression ice-cold, as she looked at Vikram. "Prepare the next phase. The time for games is over."

Back at the Safehouse:

The tension in the room was palpable as Kai, Ioanna, and Rehaan worked through the clues. There was no time for small talk; every second mattered.

Kai looked at Rehaan, his mind racing. "I need your help. Whoever's behind this isn't just after us—they're controlling everything. They've got people on the inside, they're using power and influence to cover their tracks. And it's all connected to a woman named Meera Khanna."

Rehaan's face went pale at the mention of the name. "Meera Khanna? You're telling me we're going up against her?"

"You know her?" Ioanna asked, finally speaking up.

Rehaan's jaw clenched. "Everyone in the underworld knows her. She's the kind of woman you don't cross unless you have a death wish. If she's behind this, we're in deeper trouble than I thought."

Kai nodded grimly. "Which is why we have to act fast. She's playing us, making us dance to her tune. But we need to flip the game. There's something she wants, something she's hiding. And I think the answer lies in that hotel."

Rehaan leaned in, his eyes narrowing. "You're thinking we missed something?"

"Exactly," Kai replied. "The murder wasn't just random. The person who was killed—they weren't the target. It was a message. Someone wanted us to notice something specific."

He turned to Ioanna, his eyes filled with determination. "Remember that briefcase? The one the victim had with him?"

Ioanna nodded. "Yes, but the police didn't find anything inside. It was empty."

Kai's lips curled into a knowing smile. "That's because they weren't looking in the right place. Rehaan and I once worked a case where the key evidence was hidden inside the lining of a briefcase. I bet that's where the answer is."

Rehaan's eyes lit up. "You're right. We need to get back to that hotel, find the briefcase, and see what's inside."

The Storm Intensifies:

As the storm outside grew fiercer, Kai, Ioanna, and Rehaan braced themselves for the next step. They knew Meera Khanna would not rest until she had what she wanted, and time was running out.

Kai loaded his gun, the weight of it feeling familiar in his hand. He looked at Rehaan, then at Ioanna. "We go tonight."

Rehaan nodded, his expression serious. "Let's finish this."

But deep down, Ioanna felt the growing fear—Meera Khanna was not just any villain. She was a force of nature, and they were walking right into the storm.

Puzzle Piece:

As they reached the hotel under the cover of darkness, they slipped past security and made their way to the crime scene. Everything was eerily quiet, the tension thick in the air.

Kai found the briefcase where the victim had dropped it. With precision, he and Rehaan carefully cut open the lining. Inside, they found a small, encrypted hard drive—a piece of technology so advanced, only a few people in the world could decrypt it.

Kai looked up, his eyes narrowing. "This is it. The key to everything."

Rehaan took it from his hand, his brow furrowed. "Meera's entire empire might be hidden in here."

But before they could take another step, a shadow loomed over them. A cold voice echoed through the room.

"I wouldn't touch that if I were you."

They turned slowly, and there stood Meera Khanna herself, flanked by armed men. Her eyes were cold and calculating, her smile venomous.

"You thought you could outsmart me?" she purred, stepping forward.

Rehaan took a deep breath, his eyes reflecting the admiration he had for Kai. As they stood in the dimly lit room, surrounded by a wall of evidence, Rehaan's voice grew more intense, filled with reverence as he began to recount his history with Kai.

"Kai," Rehaan started, his tone low but filled with emotion, "he's not like anyone else I've ever worked with. His mind works in ways most people can't even begin to comprehend. Every detail, every clue, no matter how small—it's like he sees the world in layers, peeling back each one until the truth is bare in front of him."

Ioanna listened carefully, curiosity piqued. She had seen Kai work his magic, but hearing it from someone else added a new layer to his legend.

Rehaan continued, his voice tightening as he recalled their first encounter. "I first met Kai during a case that was haunting the entire city—the Unrolled Book case. It was unlike anything I had ever seen. A series of murders, each one more terrifying than the last, and each victim found clutching a book... with pages missing."

Ioanna's eyes widened. "The Unrolled Book case? I heard about that... it was all over the news."

Rehaan nodded. "Yeah, it was a nightmare. People were terrified. And the worst part? No one could make sense of the clues left behind. The police were running in circles. That's when Kai stepped in."

He paused, a flicker of respect in his eyes. "At first, I didn't trust him. He was young, quiet, kept to himself. But that quiet was where his power came from. It was the way he thought—always five steps ahead of everyone else. While we were all caught up in the obvious details, Kai was already analyzing the hidden connections."

Ioanna leaned forward, hanging on to every word. "What did he do? How did he solve it?"

Rehaan's face darkened as he remembered the case. "There was this one clue... a torn page, something everyone else thought was just part of the chaos. But Kai, he noticed that the tear was deliberate. He didn't see it as damage—he saw it as a message. It led us to a hidden text, one that had been encrypted in the missing pages."

Ioanna's heartbeat quickened as Rehaan's story unfolded. She could picture Kai, the calm exterior masking the relentless wheels turning in his mind.

"From there," Rehaan continued, "Kai began to unravel everything. Each victim, each location—they weren't random. They were connected, like chapters in a story that only he could read. He figured out that the killer was leaving clues in the missing pages of the books, creating a narrative. It wasn't until Kai pieced it together that we realized... the killer wasn't just murdering people, he was writing his own twisted story."

Ioanna shivered, the weight of the story settling over her.

"How did it end?" she asked, her voice barely above a whisper.

Rehaan sighed, glancing at Kai, who was deep in thought, mapping out their current case. "It ended with a chase—one of the most intense I've ever been a part of. The killer had kidnapped someone close to me, leaving behind just one more clue. Kai tracked him down to an abandoned library, and... that's when I knew I could trust him with my life."

Rehaan's voice grew quieter, but there was a fierce pride in his words. "Kai walked in alone. Unarmed. He out-thought the killer, talked him into giving up the hostage without firing a single shot. But just when we thought it was over, the killer lunged at him."

Rehaan clenched his fists, the memory still fresh. "That's when Kai used his gun for the first time. It wasn't out of fear, though. It was a calculated move. He knew the exact moment when there was no other option. One shot—right in the leg, disarming the killer and saving everyone. That was the day I knew... Kai wasn't just good. He was the best. And he earned my respect in that instant."

Ioanna felt her heart swell with pride. Hearing Rehaan describe Kai in such vivid detail made her see him in a new light.

Rehaan glanced at Ioanna. "You know, he's not just a detective. He's a protector. And that's why I'm here today—because when Kai calls, I know something big is going down. And I trust him to see it through."

Ioanna nodded slowly, her heart full of admiration for the man she loved.

Just then, Kai turned to face them, his eyes sharp, the puzzle in front of him falling into place. "It's time," he said, his voice steady but filled with urgency. "We have to move fast. The final piece of the puzzle is almost in play."

A slow, deliberate clap echoed through the room, breaking the tense silence. The sound was unsettling, like the beginning of a twisted game no one saw coming. Both Kai and Rehaan turned sharply toward the source, and there she stood— Merra Khanna, the woman who had slipped into their investigation like a shadow.

An eerie smile curling her lips. Her hands came together again in a mocking applause, her dark eyes fixed on Rehaan.

"Well, well," Merra drawled, her voice dripping with disdain, "that was quite the touching story, Rehaan. Your friend Kai truly is remarkable... or so you'd like to believe."

Rehaan's eyes narrowed as he took a step forward. "What are you doing here, Merra? You're not supposed to be anywhere near this investigation."

Merra laughed softly, her voice laced with venom. "You think you're still in control, don't you? But here's the truth—Kai can't protect you anymore. In fact," she tilted her head slightly, her smile widening, "he never could."

Rehaan stiffened, and Ioanna felt her pulse quicken. Something was horribly wrong. The confidence Rehaan had just displayed began to waver, and Merra could sense it. She stepped into the room, her movements slow and deliberate, her presence suffocating.

Kai's expression remained calm, but Ioanna could see his eyes hardening, already calculating the next move. Merra's words hung in the air like a dark cloud, spreading doubt.

Merra's gaze flicked to Kai, her eyes gleaming with twisted satisfaction. "You've been so busy chasing ghosts, piecing together your little puzzles, but you never once saw the real game being played, did you? All this time, you've been one step behind... and now, you're about to lose everything."

Rehaan's breath caught in his throat as Merra's words sank in. His mind raced—how did she know about Kai's plans? How had she slipped through their defenses so easily?

Merra continued, her voice soft yet menacing. "Do you want to know the truth, Rehaan? Kai may have saved you once, but tonight? You're on your own. Your hero won't be able to protect you from what's coming."

The lights flickered above them, casting eerie shadows along the walls. Ioanna felt a chill crawl up her spine. This was no longer a case of outsmarting a criminal—this was something far darker, something that went beyond their understanding.

Kai stepped forward, his voice like steel. "What have you done, Merra?"

Merra chuckled, and it was a sound that sent shivers through the room. She moved closer to Rehaan, her eyes gleaming with malicious intent. "What have I done? Oh, Kai, I haven't done anything. I've merely set the stage. The pieces were already in place, and now..." she paused, her smile widening, "now it's time to see how well you really play the game."

Without warning, the lights flickered once more and then went out completely, plunging the room into total darkness. Ioanna gasped, her heart hammering in her chest. She could feel the tension, the fear rising in the air.

In the pitch-black silence, Merra's voice echoed, mocking and cold. "It's over, Kai. You've already lost. You just don't know it yet."

Suddenly, a gunshot rang out—a single, sharp crack that split the darkness. Ioanna's breath caught in her throat. There was no way to know who had fired the shot or who had been hit.

For a few agonizing seconds, there was nothing but silence.

Then, slowly, the lights flickered back on, revealing the scene before them. Kai stood at the center, his gun drawn, the barrel still smoking. But something was wrong. Rehaan was on the floor, clutching his shoulder, blood seeping through his fingers. Merra stood over him, a cruel smile on her lips.

Ioanna's heart pounded in her chest, confusion swirling in her mind. "How... how is this happening?"

Merra's gaze locked onto Kai. "You thought you had it all figured out, didn't you? But you forgot one crucial thing, Kai. In every game, there's always someone pulling the strings."

She stepped back, letting the weight of her words sink in. "You've been so focused on solving the puzzle, but you never stopped to think—what if the puzzle was designed to be unsolvable?"

Kai's eyes narrowed, his mind racing. The pieces of the puzzle—the investigation, the crime scenes, the clues—they had all been leading him to this moment. But now, he could see the truth. It wasn't just about solving a crime. Merra had been manipulating everything from the start, twisting reality, leading them into a trap.

"Rehaan," Kai called, his voice steady but urgent, "we're not done yet. This isn't over."

Rehaan struggled to his feet, his face pale but determined. "I'm with you, Kai. We'll finish this."

Merra's laughter echoed through the room. "Oh, how touching. But you're already too late. The game is almost over, and I've already won."

Kai's grip tightened on his gun as he locked eyes with Merra. "You think you've won? You haven't even seen what I'm capable of yet."

Kai's gaze locked onto Ioanna's, their silent communication taking over in the midst of the chaos. A flick of his hand—a secret gesture only they understood—passed between them, almost unnoticed by the others. Ioanna's breath caught as she realized what Kai was asking her to do. Her pulse quickened, but she stayed composed.

Without missing a beat, Kai shifted ever so slightly, keeping Merra's attention on him. With one smooth motion, he pressed his gun into Ioanna's hand, still hidden from Merra's view. Ioanna slipped back into the shadows, unnoticed by Merra, who continued to mock Kai.

"Oh, Kai," Merra sneered, her voice thick with venom. "You think you're clever. But your time is running out. You can't save everyone."

Her words hung in the air like a curse. But Kai wasn't finished—not yet.

The lights suddenly cut out, plunging the room into complete darkness. The tension was suffocating, every second stretching longer than the last. For a moment, there was nothing—no sound, no movement, just the oppressive weight of the unknown.

Then, the crack of a gunshot echoed through the room.

The silence that followed was deafening, as though the world had stopped to hold its breath. No one moved. No one dared to breathe. For an agonizing moment, it was impossible to tell who had fired—or where the bullet had struck.

Then came the sound of something metallic clattering to the floor, the bullet having ricocheted off an unseen surface. No screams. No blood. Just confusion.

Merra let out a low, sinister laugh, convinced that she still had control. "You missed, Kai."

But then, a light flickered on, illuminating a scene Merra hadn't anticipated.

Ioanna stood behind her, the gun trained on the back of her head. Kai's plan had worked flawlessly. Merra's confident smirk faltered as she realized how badly she had underestimated them.

Kai stepped forward, his voice calm yet dangerous. "You forgot one thing, Merra. I never work alone."

Ioanna's hand was steady, her gaze unwavering. Merra was trapped, her arrogance now replaced with the icy grip of fear. For the first time, she understood that the game was slipping out of her control.

Before she could respond, Ioanna's voice cut through the tension. "You're done. It's over."

But Merra wasn't ready to give up. With a sudden, desperate move, she lunged toward Ioanna, trying to grab the gun. But Ioanna was faster, stepping aside just in time. In the blink of an eye, Kai moved in, disarming Merra with surgical precision. The once-dominant villain was now defenseless, cornered in her own game.

Rehaan, injured but standing strong, smiled grimly. "Kai... I should've known you always have a backup plan."

Kai gave a slight chuckle, his eyes still locked on Merra, who was visibly shaken. "She told a good story, Rehaan. But the problem with her story is that I don't play by the rules."

Merra's cold demeanor faltered further, but she tried to regain control. "It's not over, Kai. You haven't won. This was just one piece of the puzzle."

Suddenly, the floor beneath them trembled. A loud crash echoed through the room as a hidden passageway was revealed. Merra's escape plan. Before anyone could stop her, she vanished into the dark void, her voice echoing eerily.

"This is just the beginning, Kai. You haven't seen what I'm truly capable of."

The room fell silent once again, the weight of her words hanging ominously. Kai stood still, tension rolling off him in waves. Ioanna approached him, the gun still in her hand, her expression filled with both relief and concern.

"We need to move fast," Kai said, his voice barely above a whisper.

The tension in the air thickened, every heartbeat like a countdown to something unknown. Kai, eyes narrowed, quickly scanned the room for any hint of Merra's escape route. His mind raced, piecing together the fragments of the puzzle she'd left behind. There was more to this than just her fleeing. She was playing a deeper game, and Kai knew it.

The hidden passage gaped open in front of them, a dark void leading into the unknown. Ioanna gripped the gun tighter, her hand trembling ever so slightly, though she tried to mask her fear.

"Kai," she whispered, "where does that lead?"

"I don't know yet, but I have a feeling it's not where she's really going," he said, his tone calm but calculated. His eyes darted to Rehaan, who leaned heavily on the wall, catching his breath but keeping his composure. "We need to think. Merra is always two steps ahead."

Rehaan nodded, pain etched on his face, but determination burning in his eyes. "We've been through worse, but this... something feels different this time."

Kai's mind was already working, the gears turning. He stepped toward the passage, his instincts telling him it was bait—a trap set to lure them deeper into her game. "She wants us to follow her," he murmured, "but this doesn't feel right."

Just then, a soft click echoed through the room, and Kai froze. The sound was faint, barely noticeable, but to him, it was unmistakable. A pressure-sensitive trigger had been activated— by stepping near the passageway, he had set something in motion.

Without warning, the lights flickered again, casting eerie shadows across the room. Ioanna took a step closer to him, her voice strained, "What is it?"

"A bomb," Kai whispered, his face deadly serious. "She's rigged the room."

The realization hit hard. Merra wasn't just trying to escape; she was trying to bury them alive.

"We need to get out—now!" Kai barked, his voice cutting through the rising panic.

The three of them moved swiftly, but just as they turned toward the exit, the door slammed shut with a resounding clang. A series of metallic locks clicked into place, trapping them inside. Merra's voice, cold and taunting, crackled through a hidden speaker in the room.

"You didn't really think I'd let you walk away, did you, Kai? This is where your story ends."

For a moment, silence. Then, Rehaan spoke, his voice laced with urgency, "Kai, we're running out of time."

Kai's eyes darted around the room, analyzing every corner, every piece of furniture, every crack in the wall. There had to be a way out. Merra wasn't flawless—there was always a flaw in every plan, every trap. It was just a matter of finding it.

And then it hit him. The bookshelf. It wasn't just for show.

Without explaining, Kai sprinted toward it, shoving the books aside, his fingers searching for something hidden. Rehaan and Ioanna watched, tension crackling between them.

"Kai, what are you doing?" Ioanna called out, her voice tight with fear.

He didn't answer. Instead, his fingers found what he was looking for—a small, almost imperceptible latch hidden behind the row of books. With a quick pull, a panel slid open, revealing a secondary exit—a hidden tunnel.

"Go!" Kai ordered, motioning them forward.

"But what about the bomb?" Ioanna asked, glancing nervously at the timer that had just begun counting down.

Kai's lips curved into a grim smile. "Merra may be smart, but she's predictable. This is a fake-out—a decoy bomb. She wants us to panic, to make mistakes. But I know her too well."

Rehaan's eyes widened,

As the dust settled from the collapse, Kai, Ioanna, and Rehaan emerged from the tunnel into a narrow, dimly lit corridor. The shaking had ceased, but the danger was far from over. The air was thick with tension and dust, and every sound seemed amplified in the eerie silence.

Kai's mind raced. Merra had cleverly played her hand, but he wasn't about to let her win. He knew she had to be nearby, and he had a feeling that her next move would be crucial in this game of cat and mouse.

"Stay alert," Kai instructed, his voice low and urgent. "Merra wants us to chase shadows. We need to think ahead."

Ioanna nodded, her face set with determination, and Rehaan followed suit, his eyes scanning their surroundings for any sign of danger. Kai took out his flashlight, illuminating the corridor and revealing a series of old maps and documents scattered across the floor. They were likely Merra's, and they could hold the key to her whereabouts.

Rehaan picked up one of the documents and examined it closely. "These maps... they're detailed. They cover the entire area, including underground passages."

Kai's eyes lit up. "That's it. If Merra is hiding, she's using these passages to move around unnoticed. We need to find the control room where she's operating."

The team carefully followed the corridor, their footsteps echoing softly. Kai's keen instincts led them to a hidden door camouflaged against the wall. It was locked, but Kai was prepared. He pulled out a set of lockpicks and swiftly unlocked it.

Beyond the door lay a vast control room, filled with monitors displaying various parts of the facility. The walls were lined with equipment, and in the center of the room stood Merra, her back turned to them, working furiously at a console.

Kai's heart raced as he recognized the setup—Merra was controlling the facility's security and traps from here. He signaled to Ioanna and Rehaan to take positions.

Merra's concentration was intense, and she didn't notice them approaching until Kai cleared his throat. She turned around, her eyes widening in shock and then narrowing with cold fury.

"You found me," Merra said, her voice dripping with disdain. "Impressive, but it won't be enough."

Kai stepped forward, his gaze locked on her. "The game ends here, Merra. You've orchestrated every step of this, but we're putting a stop to it."

Merra smirked. "You think you've won?"

With a swift motion, Merra activated a sequence on the console. Alarms blared, and the room was bathed in a red warning light. The facility was going into lockdown.

Kai's eyes darted to the monitors, which now showed a countdown timer ticking away. "She's set the facility to self-destruct. We have minutes before everything goes up in flames."

Merra's cruel laughter echoed through the control room. "You may have found me, but escaping this will be your real challenge."

Without hesitation, Kai lunged at the console, but Merra was faster. She grabbed a gun from her belt and aimed it at Kai. "Don't even think about it."

Ioanna, quick on her feet, grabbed a nearby metal rod and swung it at Merra, knocking the gun from her hand. The weapon skidded across the floor, and Merra scrambled to retrieve it.

In the chaos, Rehaan found a backup system panel and began working to override Merra's commands. "I need a few minutes," he called out, his fingers flying over the controls.

Kai and Ioanna fought off Merra, their movements synchronized and precise. Kai's combat skills were evident as he deftly disarmed Merra and subdued her. He moved with a confidence that spoke of years of experience and training.

As the countdown continued, Rehaan managed to access the override system. The facility's alarms stopped, and the red lights dimmed. The self-destruct sequence was deactivated.

Panting heavily, Kai turned to Merra, who lay on the floor, defeated. "It's over, Merra. You're done."

Merra's eyes blazed with defiant fury. "You may have stopped me today, but there are others. This isn't the end…"

With the facility secure and the immediate threat neutralized, Kai, Ioanna, and Rehaan made their way out. They emerged into the cool night air, the tension of the past hours slowly ebbing away.

Kai looked at his companions, relief and determination in his eyes. "We did it. But remember, this is just one chapter in a much larger story."

Ioanna squeezed his hand, her eyes reflecting both pride and gratitude. "You were amazing, Kai. I knew you could do it."

Rehaan nodded, respect clear in his gaze. "I've seen many great detectives, but you... you're something else."

Kai smiled, knowing the journey was far from over. As they walked away from the wreckage, he felt a renewed sense of purpose. There were more puzzles to solve, more shadows to chase, and more truths to uncover.

-

The cool night air was a welcome relief as Kai, Ioanna, and Rehaan emerged from the facility, the weight of their harrowing ordeal slowly lifting. The facility, now silent and still, loomed behind them, a stark reminder of the chaos that had just unfolded.

Kai glanced back at the darkened building. The alarms had ceased, and the ominous red lights were gone. The self-destruct sequence was deactivated, thanks to Rehaan's quick thinking and technical prowess.

Kai looked at Ioanna, who stood beside him, her face pale but resolute. Despite the danger they had faced, there was a spark of admiration in her eyes. Kai's heart swelled with pride and relief at seeing her safe.

Rehaan, his face smeared with grime but full of respect, approached Kai. "You handled that brilliantly. I've seen many cases, but your skill and composure were something else."

Kai nodded, acknowledging the compliment with a small smile. "Thanks, Rehaan. I couldn't have done it without your help."

The three of them started walking towards the nearest safe house, their steps heavy but determined. The moonlight cast long shadows on the ground, and the cool breeze carried away the remnants of the tension they had endured.

As they walked, Kai's mind replayed the events of the past few hours. He thought about Merra Khanna, her cruel games, and the intricate puzzle she had woven. It was clear that her defeat was just one battle in a larger war. The organization she was part of, and the many pieces still left unexplained, suggested that the end was far from sight.

Ioanna, sensing Kai's thoughts, reached out and squeezed his hand. "This isn't over, is it?"

Kai looked at her, his eyes reflecting both exhaustion and resolve. "No, it's not. We've won this round, but there's much more to uncover. Merra was just a part of a bigger picture."

They arrived at the safe house, a modest but secure location. Inside, they could finally breathe a little easier. Kai took a moment to collect his thoughts and plan their next move. The fight against the unseen forces manipulating events was far from over.

Rehaan, always perceptive, sensed Kai's thoughts. "I'll help however I can. Just let me know what you need."

Kai nodded appreciatively. "Thank you, Rehaan. Your help has been invaluable."

As the night wore on, Kai, Ioanna, and Rehaan settled into the safe house, their minds still racing from the night's events. Kai sat quietly, reflecting on the journey that had brought them here. The puzzles, the dangers, and the secrets—they were all pieces of a much larger story.

"Kai..." Rehaan whispered. "Why us? What does Merra want?"

Kai's eyes narrowed as he finally began to speak. "It's not just about us," he said, his voice low and steady. "This whole time, we've been playing a part in something much larger than we knew."

Ioanna, now standing beside them, looked at him with concern. "What are you saying?"

Kai continued, "Merra doesn't care about us as individuals. This was never personal. The moment we started digging into that old case—the 'Unrolled Book'—we stepped on the toes of powerful people. People who don't want the truth to come out."

Rehaan's jaw clenched as the gravity of the situation dawned on him. "So, this was all about silencing us?"

Kai nodded. "Exactly. We've been uncovering pieces of a conspiracy—something bigger than we imagined. The syndicate behind Merra, they have connections everywhere, and they'll do whatever it takes to protect their secrets."

Ioanna's voice was quiet but determined. "And Merra? She's part of this syndicate?"

Kai shook his head. "She's just a pawn. A dangerous one, but a pawn nonetheless. Someone is pulling her strings—someone who's been watching us closely."

Rehaan's fists tightened. "So we were targeted because we got too close?"

"Yes," Kai said, his voice firm. "This was about control. They wanted to scare us, to make sure we didn't go any further. But now..." His eyes burned with resolve. "Now, we know too much. And that makes us their biggest threat."

Ioanna placed a hand on Kai's arm. "So, what happens next?"

Kai's lips curled into a grim smile. "We take the fight to them."

Ioanna, noticing Kai's introspective mood, placed a comforting hand on his shoulder. "Whatever comes next, we'll face it together. We've proven that we're stronger than any challenge."

Kai turned to her, his expression softening. "Yes, together. And with each step, we'll get closer to the truth."

As dawn broke, casting a golden light over the safe house, a new chapter began to unfold. Kai and Rehaan made a decision that would reshape their lives: they would open a personal office for crime investigation. It was a bold move, marking the start of a new phase in their careers and lives.

A few weeks later, Kai, Ioanna, and Rehaan packed up their lives and relocated to London. The bustling city offered new opportunities and challenges, a fresh start for their crime investigation firm. Their new office, sleek and modern, was equipped with the latest technology and tools, symbolizing their commitment to unraveling the most complex cases.

In their new London office, the air was filled with anticipation. Kai and Rehaan worked tirelessly to set up their new base of operations, their minds already racing with possibilities. They knew that London's dark alleys and shadowy figures would present their own set of mysteries and dangers.

But as they settled into their new life, a chilling message arrived, delivered in a cryptic envelope. It was a warning from an anonymous source, hinting at a new threat lurking in the shadows. The message was clear: the game was far from over, and the dangers of the past were only the beginning.

Kai stared at the message, a steely determination in his eyes. He knew that the challenges ahead would test every limit and every skill he had. The journey was far from over, and the stakes were higher than ever.

As the sun set over London, casting long shadows over the city, Kai, Ioanna, and Rehaan prepared for the battles to come. The new chapter in their lives had begun, and with it, a new set of mysteries awaited.

Chapter 4

The Hunt Begins

London's skyline sparkled under the twilight, a blend of historical charm and modern grandeur. The Thames flowed quietly beneath the city's shimmering lights, and the evening mist added a touch of mystery to the streets. In the heart of this bustling metropolis, Kai Starling and his wife, Ioanna Starling, had settled into a new life.

Kai Starling had gained a reputation in London as a private detective with a sharp mind and an unyielding resolve. The city buzzed with stories of his uncanny ability to crack complex cases, earning him a place among the most respected detectives in the capital. His office, located in a sleek building near Covent Garden, was a testament to his success—modern and understated, reflecting his no-nonsense approach to crime-solving.

Ioanna, now known as Mrs. Starling, had embraced London life with a grace and enthusiasm that matched her husband's. Their home, a stylish townhouse in a quiet neighborhood, was just a short walk from Rehaan's apartment, ensuring that the trio could collaborate easily. Rehaan lived on the other side of the street, his own place a testament to his growing success as a consultant and former partner of Kai.

One crisp autumn evening, Kai took a moment to unwind on his private balcony, a vintage pipe clamped between his teeth. The pipe had become his new indulgence, a nod to old-world charm and a way to clear his mind after the day's cases. He had taken up smoking it recently, partly for the nostalgia it brought and partly for the serene moments it afforded him amidst the chaos of crime-solving.

The tranquility of the evening was abruptly interrupted by the sharp ring of the telephone. Kai's thoughts snapped back to the present as he picked up the receiver. The voice on the other end was urgent and familiar.

"Kai Starling, we need you," the voice said, revealing itself to be Inspector Alan Graves, an old acquaintance from his early days in London.

"Graves, what's the situation?" Kai asked, his tone immediately shifting to businesslike.

"There's been a high-profile case," Graves explained. "A prominent businessman was found dead under suspicious circumstances, and there's something off about the whole situation. I thought of you right away. We could use your expertise."

Kai's mind raced as he listened to the details. The case sounded like it had the potential for complexity and intrigue, just the kind of challenge he thrived on. After a brief discussion, he agreed to meet Graves at the scene.

As Kai prepared to leave, Ioanna joined him at the door, her eyes reflecting both curiosity and concern. "What's going on?" she asked.

"A new case," Kai replied, giving her a reassuring smile. "It seems like there's something unusual about this one. I'll fill you in later."

Ioanna nodded, her support unwavering. "Be careful."

Kai left for the crime scene, his thoughts already shifting to the clues and evidence he would need to examine. The night was young, and London was about to reveal another layer of its dark, enigmatic face.

At the scene, Kai was greeted by Inspector Graves, who led him into the luxurious penthouse where the businessman had been found. The room was pristine, but the tension in the air was palpable. Kai's sharp eyes took in every detail, noting the subtle signs of struggle and the odd arrangement of items in the room.

As he began his investigation, a familiar face appeared—Rehaan, who had been brought in as a consultant. "Kai, good to see you," Rehaan said, shaking his hand. "Let's get to work."

Together, Kai and Rehaan delved into the case, uncovering layers of deceit and hidden motives. They discovered that the businessman had been involved in shady dealings and had made enemies in high places. The investigation revealed connections to a secretive organization, raising the stakes of the case.

The chapter closes with Kai and Rehaan standing in the midst of the evidence, the weight of their discoveries heavy in the air. As they prepared to dig deeper, the scene was set for a thrilling confrontation with the forces at play. The mystery was far from over, and London's shadows held more secrets waiting to be uncovered.

The air in the dimly lit office crackled with tension. Detective Kai Starling's sharp eyes scanned the crime scene, a blend of focus and determination etched into his features. The room, with its scattered evidence and eerie silence, was a testament to the chilling reality of the crime that had occurred.

Inspector Collins, a seasoned veteran of the London Metropolitan Police, looked on in awe as Kai's methodical approach revealed layers of complexity in the case. Rehaan, ever the loyal partner, stood by, his expression a mix of admiration and curiosity.

Kai's gaze moved from the broken window to the overturned desk, his mind piecing together the fragments of the scene with remarkable precision. He noted the peculiar arrangement of the scattered papers and the faint, almost imperceptible traces of a struggle.

"It's not just about what's visible," Kai said, his voice calm but commanding. "It's about understanding the invisible threads that connect these clues."

Inspector Collins leaned in, intrigued. "What do you mean, Mr. Starling?"

Kai pointed to a small, almost hidden detail—a tiny smudge of red ink on the edge of a document. "This isn't random. The red ink signifies urgency and danger, a signal left deliberately. The perpetrator wanted to convey a message, but it's not obvious unless you know what to look for."

Rehaan's eyes widened. "So, what does it mean?"

Kai looked at Rehaan, a hint of a smile on his lips. "It means we're dealing with someone who's meticulous and calculating. This isn't a simple crime of passion—it's orchestrated."

Inspector Collins nodded, clearly impressed. "You're saying this was planned down to the smallest detail?"

Kai nodded. "Exactly. And the planning was so precise that it tells us the perpetrator has a deep understanding of both human psychology and criminal tactics."

As Kai continued his analysis, he began to reveal more about the crime scene's hidden aspects. He discovered a concealed compartment in the desk, containing a series of coded messages and documents linking the victim to a shadowy organization. The organization's influence stretched far beyond what anyone had anticipated.

"This organization," Kai explained, "is known for its secrecy and reach. They manipulate events from the shadows, and their involvement in this case suggests a deeper, more sinister motive."

Inspector Collins and Rehaan exchanged looks of disbelief and respect. They had witnessed Kai's skill firsthand, and it was clear that his reputation as a top-notch detective was well-earned.

Kai's phone buzzed with a new lead. He glanced at the message and turned to Rehaan and the inspector. "We have a new lead. It's time to follow this thread and see where it leads us. But be prepared—this is just the beginning."

As they prepared to leave, Kai's mind raced with the implications of the case. He knew that solving this would require more than just skill—it would demand every ounce of his determination and insight.

Kai Starling's office was filled with a focused energy as he and Rehaan delved deeper into the case. The scattered documents and evidence laid out before them were more than just clues—they were pieces of a larger, more intricate puzzle. Kai's sharp mind raced through the connections, analyzing each detail with meticulous precision.

Rehaan, who had been diligently sorting through the coded messages found in the concealed compartment, looked up from his work. "Kai, these documents point to a secret meeting scheduled for tonight. It seems like they're planning something big."

Kai's eyes narrowed as he examined the documents Rehaan handed him. "This is our break. It's likely that the meeting is crucial to understanding the full extent of this organization's plans. We need to be there."

As they prepared for the stakeout, Kai's demeanor shifted to one of intense focus. "We're not just going to observe," he said firmly. "We're going to gather evidence that will expose the full operation of this organization. This is our chance to strike a serious blow against them."

Rehaan nodded, his own determination reflecting Kai's. "I'm with you, Kai. Let's get the information we need and put an end to this."

The night was thick with anticipation as Kai and Rehaan approached the meeting location—a seemingly ordinary warehouse on the outskirts of London. The building, shrouded in darkness, concealed the dangerous activities taking place within.

Using a combination of stealth and advanced technology, Kai and Rehaan made their way inside. Kai's keen observational skills picked up on every detail—the faint hum of machinery, the hushed voices echoing through the corridors, and the faint scent of cigar smoke lingering in the air.

They navigated the maze of corridors, their footsteps silent as they approached the central meeting room. From their vantage point, they could see the key figures of the organization gathered around a table, discussing their plans with a sense of urgency.

Kai whispered to Rehaan, "This is it. We need to document everything and gather as much evidence as possible without getting caught."

As Kai and Rehaan began to record the conversation and take note of key details, the tension in the room heightened. The organization's leaders were clearly agitated, revealing plans that extended far beyond the initial crime. Their goal was to manipulate key events and individuals, ensuring their control over significant areas of influence.

Just as Kai was about to make a critical observation, a sudden noise from the entrance caught everyone's attention. The meeting room door burst open, and the atmosphere turned hostile.

The organization's security team had discovered the intruders. A tense standoff ensued as Kai and Rehaan were forced to confront the armed guards. Kai's experience and tactical skills came into play as he and Rehaan swiftly neutralized the threat.

In the chaos, Kai managed to secure a crucial piece of evidence—a dossier detailing the organization's extensive network and operations. With this, they had the information needed to dismantle the organization's grip on power.

As they made their escape, the gravity of the situation settled over them. The fight was far from over, but Kai and Rehaan had taken a significant step towards unraveling the mystery and exposing the dark forces at play.

As the adrenaline from their daring escape began to subside, Kai Starling and Rehaan made their way back to their temporary headquarters. The intensity of the night's events had taken its toll, but they found solace in the comforting routine of their office.

The office was a haven of normalcy amidst the chaos, with Kai's wife, Ioanna, and their new assistant, Emily Hart, managing the paperwork and staying on top of the day-to-day operations. Emily, a bright and diligent young woman with a knack for organization, had quickly become an invaluable part of their team. Her calm demeanor and efficiency provided a welcome contrast to the high-stress environment of their investigative work.

Ioanna, ever supportive, greeted Kai and Rehaan with a warm smile as they entered. "You two look like you've had a rough night," she remarked, her eyes filled with concern. She handed them cups of tea, the aroma of chamomile filling the room with a soothing fragrance.

Rehaan accepted the tea gratefully. "We've had a busy night, but we've made some significant progress. We've gathered evidence that could bring down the entire organization."

Emily, who had been working on organizing the evidence from the warehouse raid, looked up with a smile. "That's amazing news! I've been cross-referencing the documents with our database. We might be able to find some connections that could help us identify more of their operatives."

Kai took a seat at his desk, savoring the calming effect of the tea. "Thanks, Emily. Your help has been crucial. We wouldn't be making this progress without your support."

As the team settled into their routine, they were interrupted by the arrival of a familiar face. Detective Marcus Turner, a seasoned investigator and an old friend of Kai's, entered the office. Marcus, with his rugged demeanor and sharp wit, had been a key ally in several of Kai's past cases.

"Kai, Rehaan," Marcus greeted, shaking their hands. "I heard about your recent work. Thought I'd drop by and offer my assistance. Looks like you've got your hands full."

Kai welcomed Marcus warmly. "Glad to have you here, Marcus. We could use your expertise.

We've stumbled upon a major operation, and it's more complex than we initially thought."

As the team regrouped, Marcus's presence added a sense of camaraderie and reassurance. The discussions turned to strategies and potential leads, with Emily and Ioanna contributing their insights.

As the night wore on, the office was filled with a sense of purpose and teamwork. The shared goal of bringing justice to light and the support of their close-knit team made the weight of the investigation feel a little lighter.

Ioanna, sensing the need for a break, suggested a moment of relaxation. "Why don't we all take a brief respite? We've been working non-stop. A little time to unwind might help us think more clearly."

With a nod of agreement, the team took a short break, sharing stories and laughter. The brief respite allowed them to recharge and refocus, ready to tackle the challenges ahead.

As the team took their break, Kai Starling decided to explore another lead in London. His instincts told him that something crucial was missing from the puzzle they were trying to solve.

Kai's footsteps echoed through the bustling streets of London as he made his way to a less frequented district. The sky was beginning to darken, casting long shadows across the narrow alleyways. The vibrant lights of the city seemed a world away from the quiet, enigmatic house Kai approached.

He stood before an old, ivy-clad townhouse, its Victorian architecture hinting at a long history. This was the residence of Evelyn Blackwood, a well-known socialite with ties to the city's elite. Evelyn was rumored to have connections with some of the most influential figures in London, but her name had recently surfaced in connection with the investigation.

Kai rang the doorbell, and after a moment, Evelyn herself answered. She was elegant and composed, with an air of sophistication that matched her reputation. "Mr. Starling," she greeted him with a warm smile, though her eyes betrayed a hint of curiosity. "What brings you to my doorstep?"

Kai introduced himself and explained that he was investigating a series of high-profile crimes linked to powerful individuals. Evelyn invited him inside, offering a comfortable seat in her opulent drawing room.

As they sat down, Evelyn offered tea, and the two engaged in conversation. Kai carefully observed Evelyn's reactions and mannerisms, looking for any sign that might reveal her connection to the case.

Their conversation turned to the recent crime wave in London. Evelyn spoke with a controlled calm, but Kai noticed a flicker of concern in her eyes when he mentioned a particular detail—the pattern of the crimes and the elusive mastermind behind them.

Kai's sharp mind began to connect the dots. Evelyn's connections and her reaction to the specific details of the case suggested that she might know more than she was letting on. Kai subtly steered the conversation towards her acquaintances and any recent gatherings she might have hosted.

As the evening wore on, Evelyn's demeanor shifted slightly. She became more guarded and evasive, which only reinforced Kai's suspicions. Before he left, Evelyn mentioned a charity gala she was hosting the following weekend, an event that would be attended by many influential figures.

Kai left Evelyn's house with a growing sense of urgency. Her evasiveness and the timing of the gala seemed too convenient. He knew that this event might be the key to unraveling the mystery behind the crimes.

As Kai walked back to his car, he reviewed the new information. The gala was not just a social event; it was a potential gathering of people who could be crucial to the investigation. Kai planned to attend and observe closely.

Back at his office, Kai shared his findings with Rehaan and Ioanna. "Evelyn Blackwood is more involved than we thought. Her reaction to the details of the case and her upcoming gala might provide us with the breakthrough we need."

The team prepared for the upcoming event, knowing that the gala could be their chance to get closer to the mastermind behind the crimes. With renewed determination, they set their sights on the next phase of the investigation.

Kai Starling's mind raced as he left the scene of the crime, the echoes of Evelyn Blackwood's chilling words still reverberating in his ears. He knew there was more to this case than met the eye. The connection between the murders and the elusive mastermind had to be deeper, more intricate. Kai's reputation as a brilliant detective had always been built on his ability to see beyond the obvious, and today was no exception.

His next stop was a seemingly innocuous townhouse in a quiet part of London. The residence of a retired intelligence officer, Malcolm Hughes, who had once been a mentor to Kai. The old man had information that could crack the case wide open.

As Kai arrived, he found Malcolm seated in his study, surrounded by walls of dusty old books and maps. The room was dimly lit, casting long shadows that danced eerily with every flicker of the antique lamp. Malcolm's eyes, though tired, were sharp and analytical.

"Kai," Malcolm greeted, his voice carrying the weight of decades of experience. "I've heard about the case. You're in deep this time."

Kai took a seat across from Malcolm, the weight of his exhaustion evident in his posture. "Malcolm, I need to understand the connection between the victims. Something isn't adding up. The way they were killed... it's too calculated."

Malcolm leaned forward, his eyes narrowing. "You're looking at it from the wrong angle. This isn't just about the murders. It's about the power dynamics in London. The elite, the power struggles—they're all intertwined. The true crime isn't just what happened, but why it happened."

Kai absorbed Malcolm's words, feeling the pieces of the puzzle shifting. "So you're saying the mastermind isn't just targeting individuals but is sending a message to a larger audience?"

Malcolm nodded. "Precisely. The mastermind is using these murders as a tool to manipulate and control. The charity gala is the key. It's a stage for their next move."

With newfound determination, Kai left Malcolm's house and headed to the gala venue. The event was in full swing, the opulence and grandeur belying the sinister undercurrents that Kai knew lurked beneath. Guests mingled, laughter and clinking glasses filled the air, but Kai's focus was razor-sharp.

As he moved through the crowd, he spotted a familiar face—one that hadn't been there before. A striking woman in an elegant red dress, her eyes darting around nervously. Kai approached her with careful precision.

"Miss Blackwood," he said, his voice calm but authoritative. "May I have a word?"

Evelyn Blackwood's face went pale, her composure slipping. "Detective Starling," she said, her voice trembling slightly. "I'm afraid I don't have much to say."

Kai studied her closely, noting the anxiety in her eyes. "The murders you're connected to—there's more to them than what's on the surface. You're hiding something."

Evelyn's lips quivered, but she remained silent. The tension between them was palpable, a silent battle of wills. Kai knew he was close to uncovering the truth, but he needed more.

As the gala continued, Kai's mind raced with theories and possibilities. The connection between the victims, the manipulation, the power struggle—it was all starting to fall into place. But just as he was about to make his move, a commotion erupted near the entrance. The lights flickered, casting eerie shadows over the crowd.

Suddenly, Evelyn screamed, her voice filled with terror. Kai's heart pounded as he raced toward the source of the disturbance. A figure was seen fleeing through a side door, disappearing into the night.

Kai chased after the figure, his instincts guiding him through the maze of alleyways and darkened streets. Finally, he cornered the suspect in an abandoned warehouse. The confrontation was intense, a battle of wits and willpower. The suspect, a hired gun working for the mastermind, revealed crucial details before being apprehended.

The truth began to emerge, piecing together the complex web of deception and power that had driven the murders. Kai's relentless pursuit of justice was paying off, but the mastermind's ultimate goal remained shrouded in mystery.

As the chapter drew to a close, Kai and Rehaan, now reunited, prepared for the next phase of their investigation. The stage was set for a high-stakes showdown, with the future of London's elite hanging in the balance.

The tension was palpable, the psychological games intensifying. Kai knew that every move from here on out had to be calculated with precision. The game was far from over, and the stakes had never been higher.

Back at the gala, the scene was still chaotic. The inspector, a rather befuddled gentleman named Inspector Douglas Bennett, was trying his best to make sense of the confusion. He had been called in to handle the aftermath of the disturbance, but his understanding of the situation was as tangled as the strands of the investigation itself.

Kai Starling approached Inspector Bennett, his expression a mix of amusement and frustration. The inspector was busy jotting down notes, but his confusion was evident.

"Inspector Bennett," Kai began, "I think it's time we had a little chat about what's really going on here."

The inspector looked up, his brow furrowed. "Yes, Mr. Starling, please enlighten me. I'm still trying to piece together what happened."

Kai cleared his throat and launched into a detailed explanation. "Alright, so the sequence of events starts with the fact that the mastermind orchestrated these murders to send a message to London's elite. The gala was a strategic move, a stage for their next plan. Evelyn Blackwood is not just a socialite; she's a key player in this intricate game. The figure who fled—"

The inspector interrupted, scratching his head. "Wait, wait, wait. So, you're telling me this was all planned out like a chess game?"

Kai nodded, a faint smile playing on his lips. "Precisely. The mastermind used these murders as a message to manipulate and control the elite. The gala was the perfect cover."

Inspector Bennett blinked, his jaw dropping as he tried to process the information. "So you're saying this is all about power and control? And the gala was just a ruse?"

Kai's smile widened. "Exactly. And the suspect who fled was actually a hired gun working for the mastermind. We've got the whole puzzle laid out now."

The inspector's eyes widened further. "Good heavens, Mr. Starling, you're telling me I've been chasing my own tail? I thought it was just a string of unfortunate events!"

Kai chuckled softly. "You could say that. It's a bit more elaborate than that."

Inspector Bennett shook his head in disbelief. "I've got to hand it to you, Starling. You've got a mind like a steel trap. I never would have figured this out on my own."

Kai gave him a reassuring nod. "Well, that's why we make a good team. Now let's get to work on the next steps."

As they walked away from the scene, Inspector Bennett's expression was a mixture of awe and embarrassment. He had seen many cases in his time, but this one was shaping up to be one of the most complex he had ever encountered. And with Kai Starling on the case, he had a newfound respect for the detective's unparalleled skills.

"Just don't expect me to keep up with you all the time," the inspector joked, a sheepish grin spreading across his face.

Kai laughed. "Don't worry, Inspector. I'm sure we'll have plenty of time to get you up to speed."

With that, Kai and the inspector set off, their steps echoing through the grand hall of the gala. The game was still afoot, but with every twist and turn, Kai's confidence grew. The investigation was far from over, and he was ready to tackle whatever came next.

The night deepened, Kai Starling found himself alone in his office, the dim glow of the desk lamp casting long shadows across the room. The grandeur of London outside seemed a world away from the quiet intensity within. Kai leaned back in his leather chair, a contemplative expression on his face.

He pulled out his pipe, lighting it with a practiced hand. The rich, aromatic smoke curled lazily into the air, mingling with the faint notes of cedarwood and old books that filled the room. Kai stared at the swirling smoke, lost in thought.

The gala's chaotic scene replayed in his mind. Every detail, every subtle nuance of the crime, was etched clearly in his memory. The elegance of Evelyn Blackwood's house, the suspicious behavior of the guests, and the haunting look in the eyes of the fleeing suspect—all of it formed a puzzle that was slowly coming together.

Kai took a deep drag from his pipe, the familiar warmth calming his mind. He thought about the intricate web of deception and power that had been woven around London's elite. The mastermind behind the murders was a formidable opponent, but Kai felt a surge of determination. He would not rest until the truth was uncovered.

As he exhaled a plume of smoke, he contemplated the next steps. The pieces of the puzzle were falling into place, but there were still gaps that needed to be filled. He needed to delve deeper into Evelyn Blackwood's connections, scrutinize the motives of the suspects, and uncover the true agenda behind the crimes.

Kai's thoughts were interrupted by a knock on the door. Rehaan entered, his expression serious but tinged with curiosity.

"Kai," Rehaan said, "you've been in here for hours. What's on your mind?"

Kai looked up, a thoughtful smile on his lips. "Just piecing together the final details. There's a lot more to this case than meets the eye. The mastermind is using these crimes as a way to manipulate and control. Evelyn Blackwood's role is crucial, and we need to understand her connections better."

Rehaan nodded, his interest piqued. "I've been doing some digging myself. There are some interesting leads about Blackwood's associates. We might be able to make a breakthrough if we follow up on them."

Kai took one last drag from his pipe before extinguishing it. "Excellent. Let's follow those leads and see where they take us. The sooner we get to the bottom of this, the better."

As the two men prepared to dive back into the investigation, Kai's mind remained focused on the intricate layers of deception they were unraveling. The city of London was full of shadows and secrets, but with each step they took, the truth became clearer.

With renewed resolve, Kai and Rehaan set off into the night, ready to confront the next challenge in their quest for justice. The mystery was far from solved, but Kai Starling was determined to see it through to the end.

Kai Starling, resolute in his pursuit of justice, began mapping out his strategy for the next phase of the investigation. Each step was meticulously planned, his sharp mind piecing together the complex tapestry of the case.

His first move took him back to Evelyn Blackwood's mansion, where he intended to explore the opulent but enigmatic environment further. The mansion, with its grand chandeliers and ornate decor, seemed to hide more secrets behind its luxurious facade. Kai approached with caution, knowing that appearances could be deceiving.

Inside, he was greeted by Evelyn, her demeanor composed but with an underlying tension. "Mr. Starling," she said, her voice smooth but guarded, "to what do I owe the pleasure?"

"I'm here to delve deeper into the recent events," Kai replied, his tone professional but assertive. "I need to understand more about your connections and any recent disturbances."

Evelyn led him to her private study, a room filled with rare books and historical artifacts. As they spoke, Kai's keen eyes observed every detail— an expensive letter opener here, a carefully curated painting there. He noted the subtle signs of anxiety in Evelyn's posture and the way she shifted her gaze.

After a thorough discussion, Kai exited the mansion with a clear sense of Evelyn's mounting pressure. He headed to a less glamorous, yet equally significant location: the city's renowned club where influential figures congregated. This club, frequented by London's elite, might hold vital clues about the case.

Inside the club, Kai mingled with guests, adopting a casual, unassuming manner. He engaged in conversations, subtly probing for information. The club's owner, a man named Geoffrey Langford, seemed particularly nervous. Kai's instincts told him that Geoffrey might know more than he was letting on.

Kai approached Geoffrey discreetly. "Mr. Langford, I understand this may be a sensitive topic, but have you noticed any unusual activities or guests recently?"

Langford's face paled slightly, but he managed to maintain his composure. "I can't say I've seen anything out of the ordinary, Mr. Starling. This is a place for discretion, after all."

Kai, unfazed, nodded thoughtfully. "Of course. Thank you for your time."

As Kai left the club, he noticed a shadowy figure watching him from across the street. The figure quickly vanished into the night, fueling Kai's suspicions. He decided to follow the trail, leading him to a nondescript warehouse on the edge of the city.

Inside the warehouse, Kai and Rehaan discovered a hidden room filled with documents, photographs, and files detailing the lives of various high-profile individuals. It became clear that the warehouse was a hub for illicit activities, and the mastermind behind the crimes had been using it to orchestrate their plans.

Kai's analytical mind raced through the information. He pieced together the connections between the victims and the clues he had gathered. It was evident that the crimes were not random but part of a larger scheme to control and manipulate powerful figures.

The night was closing in, and Kai knew that time was of the essence. With the evidence collected, he prepared to confront Evelyn Blackwood and other key players involved. The next steps in his plan would be crucial in exposing the truth and bringing the perpetrators to justice.

As dawn approached, Kai and Rehaan stood on the brink of unraveling the final pieces of the puzzle. Their resolve was unwavering, and they were ready to face whatever challenges lay ahead.

--

Kai Starling's investigation had reached a critical juncture. With the evidence gathered from the warehouse, he was prepared for the final confrontation. His target was a notorious criminal named Victor Holloway, known for his cunning and ruthlessness. Holloway was suspected to be the linchpin in the criminal network orchestrating the high-profile murders.

Kai tracked Holloway to a dingy apartment on the outskirts of London. The place was a stark contrast to the opulence of the city's elite, reflecting Holloway's fall from grace. Kai and Rehaan entered the dimly lit room, where Holloway was sitting nervously, his eyes darting between them and the door.

Holloway looked up, fear evident in his eyes. "Mr. Starling," he said, his voice trembling. "What brings you here?"

Kai's presence was commanding. He took a slow step forward, his gaze unwavering. "Victor Holloway, you're under arrest for your involvement in a series of high-profile crimes. The evidence against you is substantial."

Holloway's demeanor shifted from defiance to desperation. "Please, Mr. Starling, you don't understand. I was forced into this. They have threatened my family. I didn't have a choice."

Kai's expression remained impassive. "You can save your excuses for the court. However, if you cooperate fully and provide us with all the information you have, it might work in your favor."

Holloway gulped, nodding vigorously. "I'll tell you everything. Just please, let me go. I'll leave London and never come back. I just need to protect my family."

Kai's gaze narrowed. "You'll be handed over to the authorities, but if you cooperate, I'll make sure your cooperation is noted. But remember, any falsehoods or omissions will not be tolerated."

Holloway's shoulders slumped in defeat as Kai handed him over to the waiting inspector. The inspector, stunned by the turn of events, took Holloway into custody.

The scene shifted to a private room at the police headquarters, where Kai, Rehaan, and the inspector gathered. Holloway, now subdued, began to spill details about the criminal network, revealing how he was coerced into the crimes by a powerful syndicate led by Evelyn Blackwood.

He detailed their operations and provided critical leads on the remaining members of the network.

Holloway's confession also included a chilling admission that the syndicate planned to expand their operations beyond London, targeting other cities with their sinister agenda. His plea for leniency was earnest, and he provided Kai with enough information to dismantle the criminal network.

Kai listened intently, absorbing every detail. "Thank you for your cooperation, Victor. Your information will be crucial in bringing the others to justice. Remember, your fate depends on the truth you've shared here."

As Holloway was escorted away, Kai turned to Rehaan and the inspector. "We have a lead on the remaining members of the syndicate. The next steps are crucial. We need to act swiftly to prevent further damage."

The inspector, awed by Kai's methodical approach and the unraveling of the criminal network, nodded in agreement. "Mr. Starling, your skills are extraordinary. We couldn't have reached this point without your expertise."

Kai, satisfied with the progress but knowing the case was far from over, prepared for the next phase of the investigation. His resolve was unwavering, and the shadow of the criminal syndicate loomed large.

With Holloway's revelations, Kai and his team were now better equipped to confront the larger conspiracy and bring the remaining criminals to justice. The battle was far from over, but Kai Starling was determined to see it through to the end.

As Holloway was escorted out, Rehaan turned to Kai with a look of curiosity and admiration. "Kai, that was impressive. But I have to ask—how did you find Holloway so quickly? It seemed like you were always one step ahead."

Kai took a contemplative drag from his pipe, the smoke curling into the air as he began to explain. "It's a matter of piecing together the clues and understanding the patterns of behavior. Holloway has been on the fringes of the criminal underworld for years. He's known for his desperation and fear, which made him a prime target for manipulation."

He continued, "I noticed a pattern in the communication and movements of the syndicate. They were cautious, but Holloway's fear made him slip. His pattern was inconsistent compared to others in the network, which made him easier to track. His recent activities indicated a retreat, likely in anticipation of us closing in."

Rehaan's eyes widened with realization. "So you used his fear and desperation against him, while also tracking the syndicate's broader movements. That's brilliant. Bravo, Kai!"

Kai offered a slight, satisfied smile. "Thank you, Rehaan. It's all about understanding the psychology of the individuals involved and the network as a whole. Now that we have Holloway's confession, we can move forward with targeting the core members of the syndicate."

The inspector, who had been listening intently, nodded in agreement. "Mr. Starling, your methods are truly remarkable. We're fortunate to have you on this case."

Kai's gaze turned resolute. "This is just the beginning. We have a lot of work ahead of us, but with the information we've gathered, we're in a strong position to dismantle this network. Let's not waste any time."

With that, Kai, Rehaan, and the inspector prepared to dive deeper into the investigation, their resolve strengthened by the progress made. The path ahead was fraught with challenges, but they were ready to face them head-on, determined to bring the criminal syndicate to justice.

As the sun dipped below the horizon, casting long shadows across London, Kai Starling's mind raced with the details of the case. Each piece of evidence, each clue, began to form a clearer picture. He knew the final steps were crucial; this was where the true test of his skills would come into play.

Kai and Rehaan sat in the dimly lit office, the air heavy with tension. Kai's pipe smoldered quietly beside him as he reviewed the latest intel. His eyes, sharp and focused, scanned through the documents and photographs spread across the table. Every detail was vital, and he was determined to leave nothing to chance.

The door creaked open, and a young detective named Clara entered. "Mr. Starling, we've received a lead on the location of the syndicate's central meeting place. It's a derelict warehouse on the outskirts of the city. They've been spotted there multiple times."

Kai's expression remained stoic, but a flicker of anticipation danced in his eyes. "Perfect. It's time we put an end to this."

As they approached the warehouse, the night air grew colder, and the fog rolled in, shrouding the area in an eerie silence. Kai and Rehaan moved with practiced stealth, their footsteps muffled by the thick fog. The warehouse loomed ahead, a dark, foreboding structure against the night sky.

Kai signaled for them to stop. "We need to be cautious. The syndicate will be on high alert."

They crept closer, the only sound being the distant hum of city life. Kai's keen eyes caught sight of movement through a cracked window. The syndicate members were gathered inside, their hushed voices and sporadic laughter betraying their sense of security.

Kai gestured to Rehaan. "This is it. We go in now, and we go in hard. We need to catch them red-handed."

With precision and speed, Kai and Rehaan made their way inside. The warehouse was dimly lit, the shadows stretching ominously as they moved through the labyrinth of crates and machinery. They could hear the murmurs of the syndicate members, their conversation growing louder as they approached.

Suddenly, a door creaked open, and the members froze, their eyes widening in shock as Kai and Rehaan stepped into view. The atmosphere was electric with tension, the air thick with anticipation.

Kai took a deep breath, his voice cutting through the silence. "It's over. Surrender now, and no one gets hurt."

The syndicate members scrambled, their faces a mix of fear and defiance. Kai's commanding presence and unwavering confidence left no room for doubt. This was the moment he had been working towards, and he was ready to see it through.

The confrontation that followed was intense, a whirlwind of action and strategy. Kai's sharp instincts and meticulous planning paid off as he and Rehaan apprehended the remaining members of the syndicate. The final pieces of the puzzle fell into place, and the network was finally dismantled.

As the dust settled and the first light of dawn began to break, Kai stood amidst the remnants of the warehouse, his gaze fixed on the horizon. The case was closed, but the thrill of the chase and the satisfaction of justice served lingered.

Rehaan approached, a look of admiration in his eyes. "You did it, Kai. You brought them down."

Kai nodded, a small, satisfied smile playing at the corners of his lips. "We did it, Rehaan. And this is just the beginning."

With the syndicate dismantled and justice served, Kai Starling and his team were ready to face whatever challenges lay ahead. The city of London had witnessed their skills, and the world would soon know the name of Kai Starling—the detective who could outwit even the most elusive criminals.

The dawn began to cast its first light over the London skyline, an unexpected sound shattered the fragile calm of the morning: the sharp crack of a gunshot.

Kai Starling, still standing amidst the scattered remnants of the warehouse, turned abruptly, his senses on high alert. The shot had come from somewhere close by, and the familiar rush of adrenaline surged through him. He and Rehaan exchanged a glance, both understanding the gravity of the situation.

"Get down!" Kai shouted, pulling Rehaan to cover behind a stack of crates.

The sound of footsteps echoed through the warehouse, a frantic scramble of movement. Kai's mind raced, piecing together the unfolding scene. Whoever had fired the shot was either making a desperate escape or attempting to sabotage their success.

With his gun drawn, Kai moved swiftly and silently through the dimly lit space. His eyes scanned every shadow, every corner, looking for any sign of the shooter. Rehaan followed closely, his own weapon ready.

The tension was palpable, the silence punctuated only by the occasional distant thud or the muffled sounds of the city waking up. Kai's sharp instincts led him toward the source of the disturbance. As he approached a side door, he could see the faint glow of a flashlight flickering through the small window.

Kai paused, listening intently. The distinct sound of someone trying to breach a lock reached his ears. He motioned for Rehaan to take position on one side of the door while he positioned himself on the other.

With a swift kick, Kai burst through the door, revealing a figure standing in the dim light, clutching a gun. The individual's face was partially hidden by a hood, but the desperation in their stance was clear.

Kai's voice was steady, authoritative. "Drop the weapon and surrender!"

The figure hesitated for a moment, their eyes darting around nervously. But before they could react, another gunshot rang out, and the figure crumpled to the ground, the gun falling from their hand.

Kai's heart raced as he scanned the area, searching for the shooter. He saw a shadow disappearing into the foggy distance.

"Rehaan, secure the area!" Kai commanded.

As Rehaan moved to handle the situation, Kai approached the fallen figure. The person's face was now visible, revealing a familiar, yet surprising, countenance. It was someone Kai had encountered in his past cases—a known associate of the syndicate, whose involvement had been a mystery until now.

Kneeling beside the unconscious figure, Kai retrieved a hidden note from their jacket pocket. The note was cryptic but hinted at another layer of the conspiracy—one that involved high-profile figures in the city, indicating that their work was far from over.

With the immediate threat neutralized, Kai took a deep breath, his mind racing to connect the dots. The gunshot was not just a random act of violence; it was a final desperate move by someone who had much more to lose. The case had taken a darker turn, revealing the depth of the corruption they were up against.

Kai and Rehaan gathered their findings and prepared to leave the warehouse. As they walked out into the early morning light, the weight of the unresolved conspiracy hung heavily over them. The threat was not yet eradicated, and the true extent of the danger remained obscured.

The city of London awaited, with its secrets and shadows, as Kai Starling and his team braced themselves for the next phase of their investigation.

--

As the echo of the gunshot faded, Kai Starling and Rehaan stood amidst the tense silence, the weight of their discovery settling heavily. Kai, his face a mask of steely determination, began to outline the chilling truth behind the murders that had gripped London.

Gathering the remaining detectives and the key figures in the investigation, Kai addressed them with a commanding presence. "The truth about this crime is far more intricate than we initially thought," he began, his voice cutting through the murmur of anticipation.

He proceeded to reveal the identities of the seven individuals behind the conspiracy:

1. Arthur Holloway - The shadowy mastermind behind the scheme, whose criminal empire spanned across continents.

2. Evelyn Blackwood - A high-profile socialite with hidden ties to Holloway, known for her manipulation of London's elite.

3. Merra Khanna - The enigmatic strategist, whose actions had orchestrated much of the chaos.

4. George Whitaker - An ex-military operative with a violent streak, employed to enforce Holloway's will.

5. Samantha Rivers - A skilled hacker who had breached numerous security systems, aiding the group's illegal activities.

6. Liam O'Connor - A corrupt official who had facilitated the group's operations by turning a blind eye to their crimes.

7. Clara Dunn - An insider within a major financial institution, whose information had been pivotal in laundering the proceeds.

Kai's revelations sent shockwaves through the room. "These seven individuals are not just culprits but the very architects of a vast criminal network," he said. "Their web of deceit has now been unraveled, and the citizens of London must know the truth."

The atmosphere in the room was electric with disbelief and awe. Kai's meticulous unraveling of the case had not only exposed the criminals but had also demonstrated the depth of his investigative prowess.

As the Londoners absorbed the gravity of the situation, a new sense of resolve filled the air. With the names of the seven known, the city braced itself for the ongoing battle against the remnants of the conspiracy.

Kai Starling's reputation as London's finest private detective was solidified, his actions ensuring that justice would prevail and that the dark shadows of the crime would be chased away.

As the room quieted, Kai Starling turned his attention to Rehaan, who had been closely following the developments. The gravity of the case had left them both on edge, and now, as the final pieces of the puzzle fell into place, Kai needed to explain the full scope of the criminal conspiracy.

"Kai," Rehaan said, his voice laced with curiosity and anticipation, "what's the motive behind all these crimes? Why did they go to such lengths?"

Kai took a deep breath, his gaze steady. "The motive behind this conspiracy is rooted in power and control. Arthur Holloway and his associates orchestrated this entire operation to establish dominance over London's financial and political elite."

He began to outline the intricate details. "Holloway's criminal empire was built on exploiting vulnerabilities within powerful institutions. Evelyn Blackwood's role was to manipulate influential figures, creating a network of power that extended into the highest echelons of society. Merra Khanna, with her strategic mind, ensured that their plans were executed flawlessly."

"Kai," Rehaan interrupted, "what was their endgame?"

"Their ultimate goal," Kai continued, "was to destabilize the financial systems and political structures of London. By creating chaos and manipulating key figures, they aimed to control major decisions and secure vast financial gains through their illicit activities. Each member of the conspiracy had a specific role that contributed to this overarching plan."

Rehaan's eyes widened with realization. "So, the murders and the crimes were all part of their strategy to cover their tracks and maintain their control?"

"Exactly," Kai confirmed. "The murders were meant to eliminate threats and keep their operations hidden. The violence and intimidation were tools to ensure compliance and silence anyone who posed a risk to their plans."

As Kai concluded his explanation, the room was filled with a tense silence. The intricate web of deceit had been laid bare, and the motives behind the crimes were now clear. The conspiracy's reach had extended far beyond what they had initially imagined, touching every corner of London's elite society.

Kai's meticulous work had not only unraveled the criminal network but had also provided a clear understanding of their motives. With this knowledge, the path forward was clear. The fight against the remnants of the conspiracy was just beginning, and the city was poised for the next chapter in its battle for justice.

As Kai and Rehaan prepared to take their next steps, the resolution of the case marked a turning point. London, now aware of the depth of the conspiracy, would face the challenge of reclaiming its integrity and ensuring that the shadows of crime were finally dispelled.

The gravity of Kai Starling's revelations settled, the room remained hushed. The weight of the criminal network's exposure was immense, but so was the resolve of those determined to see justice served.

Kai, with a calm yet resolute demeanor, addressed Rehaan. "The motive behind these crimes was not merely financial gain. It was about power, control, and maintaining dominance over London's elite. The seven were not just participants; they were pieces of a larger, more dangerous game."

Rehaan nodded, absorbing the gravity of Kai's words. "And with this understanding, what's next?"

Kai's gaze was steady, his voice unwavering. "We dismantle their network, ensure their downfall, and restore order. The city will recover from the shadows they cast, but it will take time and vigilance."

The sun began to set over London, casting long shadows across its streets, Kai and Rehaan prepared for the battles ahead. The city's secrets had been unveiled, but the path to complete justice would be a long and arduous one.

Kai turned to Rehaan with a hint of a smile. "Well, well, well, my dear Rehaan, let's drink some brandy, play the violin, and then venture to another state. We've earned a respite, and the future awaits us."

With that, Kai Starling and his team set their sights on the challenges ahead, knowing that their journey was far from over but ready to embrace the new adventures to come.

Chapter 5

The Veiled Mirage

The sun set low over the horizon as Kai Starling and his team prepared for a journey that promised to unravel a new mystery. It all started with an invitation—a simple, elegant note from an old acquaintance, Luca Mariani, a renowned art collector based in Morocco. The note was brief, but the message was clear: "I need your expertise. A masterpiece has been stolen—The Veiled Mirage—and I fear it's more than just a painting that's gone missing."

Kai, ever the one to be drawn into intrigue, leaned back in his chair, puffing thoughtfully on his pipe. "It's time, Rehaan. We're off to Morocco."

Rehaan, eager as always, smiled at the prospect of their new adventure. "What do we know about this painting, Kai? What's so special about The Veiled Mirage?"

Kai's fingers tapped the table rhythmically as he spoke. "The painting is said to be connected to an ancient secret society, with a history that runs deep into the criminal underworld. It's not just about the art, Rehaan. It's about what it represents—power, control, and the secrets it hides."

Ioanna, seated nearby, looked up from her book. "And who's Luca Mariani?"

"An old acquaintance," Kai replied with a slight smirk. "An eccentric art collector who dabbles in more than just art. He's been involved in several high-profile cases in the past, but this time, I sense something much bigger."

The trio prepared for their departure to Morocco, with Rehaan living across from Kai and Ioanna's home in London. As they boarded the plane, the tension between them was palpable. This wasn't just another case—this was something deeper, something that promised to push them to their limits.

Upon landing in Casablanca, the vibrant city welcomed them with its buzzing markets, aromatic scents, and dazzling colors. Luca Mariani was waiting, his tall frame and silver hair glinting in the evening light.

"Kai, Rehaan, Mrs. Starling," Luca greeted them warmly, shaking hands. "I'm glad you could make it. We're dealing with something that could shake the very foundations of the art world and beyond."

"What do you mean?" Ioanna asked, her curiosity piqued.

Luca's eyes darkened. "The Veiled Mirage is not just a painting. It's a key—a key to an ancient network, one that has been controlling the flow of wealth, power, and influence for centuries. Whoever has that painting holds the power to unlock a secret society that's remained hidden in the shadows for far too long."

Kai raised an eyebrow, intrigued. "And who do you suspect is behind this theft?"

Luca hesitated for a moment before answering. "Youssef Rahimi. He was once part of my security team—a former expert turned rogue. He has the connections, the knowledge, and the motive. But there's more to it than just him. I'm certain this goes deeper."

As the team began their investigation, they were introduced to other key players, including Mira Al-Hassan, an art historian with extensive knowledge of the painting's history, and Omar Fakhri, a local gallery owner with his own set of secrets.

The clues they gathered pointed them to an underground auction happening in the heart of the city, where rare and stolen artifacts were being sold to the highest bidder. But as they dug deeper, the shadows began to shift.

"This isn't just about the painting anymore," Kai said one evening as they gathered their findings. "Someone is orchestrating this entire operation. Someone with deep ties to the Crime."

The tension built as they followed the trail of clues through the narrow alleyways and hidden corners of Casablanca. Youssef Rahimi's name kept coming up, but it felt like they were being led into a trap.

"We need to tread carefully," Rehaan warned. "It feels like we're walking straight into something bigger than we anticipated."

Kai nodded, taking a slow drag from his pipe. "I agree, but we're too far in to back out now. We need to get to the bottom of this."

The chapter would end with the trio uncovering a hidden vault beneath a luxurious mansion, where the stolen painting was kept, but not before encountering a shocking betrayal from someone they thought they could trust. The cliffhanger would leave readers eagerly awaiting the next phase of their journey, as Kai, Ioanna, and Rehaan delve further into the mysteries surrounding The Veiled Mirage and the dark forces controlling it.

As they stood before the hidden vault, the air in the room thickened with tension. Kai Starling's sharp eyes flickered from the locked chamber to the figures surrounding him. He could feel the weight of something bigger than they had anticipated—a secret that had been buried for centuries, now on the verge of being exposed.

Rehaan, sensing the unease in the air, asked quietly, "Kai, do you think we're ready for what's behind that door?"

Kai took a long drag from his pipe, exhaling slowly before speaking. "We're about to find out, my dear Rehaan."

The echo of those words hung in the air as they prepared to uncover the next layer of the mystery that awaited them.

Kai Starling and Rehaan stepped out into the bustling streets of Casablanca, the Moroccan sun casting long shadows across the ancient buildings. The air was filled with the vibrant hum of the city, but Kai's focus remained razor-sharp. They had been invited by Luca Mariani, a well-known art collector, to solve the mysterious disappearance of his prized possession: a painting known as The Veiled Mirage.

As they arrived at Luca's grand estate, they were greeted by the first of many intriguing characters in their investigation.

Luca Mariani was an older man, in his late sixties, with silver hair and a distinguished air about him. Despite his wealth, there was a nervous energy beneath his calm demeanor. He welcomed them into his ornate sitting room, where the investigation would begin.

"Mr. Starling, I've heard much of your reputation," Luca said, gesturing for them to sit.

"I hope you can help me recover my lost treasure. This painting means more to me than you can imagine."

Kai nodded, his sharp eyes taking in the room and the people in it.

Standing by Luca's side was Mira Al-Hassan, an art historian with expertise in rare and ancient pieces. She had dark, piercing eyes and an enigmatic presence. Mira had been working closely with Luca for years, curating his collection, and was the one who first discovered the theft.

Next, there was Youssef Rahimi, a former security expert who had been hired to protect the estate. He was tall, muscular, and spoke little, but his deep frown suggested that he took the theft as a personal failure.

Then, there was Fatima Belkacem, Luca's assistant. She was young, in her twenties, with a sharp wit and an inquisitive mind. Her loyalty to Luca was obvious, but there was something in the way she looked at the others—an unease that Kai picked up on immediately.

As the introductions concluded, Kai and Rehaan began to ask questions, starting the investigation.

"Tell me, Luca," Kai said, his tone measured, "who knew about the painting and its exact location?"

Luca hesitated for a moment, glancing toward Mira before answering. "Only a handful of people—myself, Mira, Youssef, and Fatima. No one else knew it was being kept here, in the hidden vault."

Kai exchanged a quick look with Rehaan, the gears in his mind already turning. There was more to this theft than just a stolen painting. There was an intricate web of secrets waiting to be untangled, and he was about to pull the first thread.

The investigation began, Kai Starling decided to step back for a moment and take in the beauty of Morocco. The country held its own mysteries, and perhaps, Kai thought, inspiration for solving the case would come from embracing its enchanting landscape.

Kai, Rehaan, and Ioanna took a brief detour to explore the vibrant streets of Casablanca. The city was a blend of modernity and tradition, where ancient architecture stood proudly against the backdrop of towering skyscrapers. The Hassan II Mosque, with its intricate carvings and towering minaret, left them in awe as the golden light of the setting sun bathed the city in a warm glow.

Strolling through the Medina, they were engulfed by the intoxicating scents of Moroccan spices—cumin, cinnamon, and saffron mixing in the air. Market stalls burst with vibrant colors, showcasing handcrafted rugs, pottery, and lanterns that glittered in the sunlight. The calls of the merchants and the sound of traditional music in the background created a symphony of life.

"I always forget how breathtaking this place is," Ioanna said, smiling as she pulled Kai closer to her side.

Kai nodded, his usual serious expression softening for a moment. "It's the kind of place that lets you forget your troubles. But only for a while," he added, his thoughts quickly returning to the missing painting.

As they wandered through the Jemaa el-Fnaa in Marrakesh, the square came alive with snake charmers, storytellers, and acrobats performing before crowds of excited tourists and locals. Kai couldn't help but be fascinated by the vibrant energy of the place, though his keen eyes never stopped observing, calculating, and analyzing every detail.

The trio later visited the stunning Majorelle Garden, a peaceful oasis filled with exotic plants and vividly colored fountains. Ioanna marveled at the cobalt blue buildings, while Rehaan joked about turning their next office into something similar.

"I'm not sure how a bright blue crime investigation office would work in London," Kai quipped, lighting his pipe and taking a slow, thoughtful puff. He exhaled, watching the smoke curl into the blue Moroccan sky, his mind still dissecting the clues they had gathered so far.

As night fell, the three sat on a rooftop café, enjoying mint tea under the stars. The city's lights twinkled in the distance, and the Atlas Mountains loomed in the horizon, shadowy and mysterious. There was a beauty in the stillness of the evening that seemed to reflect the calm before the storm of their investigation.

But in Kai's mind, the pieces of the puzzle were slowly coming together. The stolen painting, the people involved, the hidden motives—it all swirled around him like the smoke from his pipe. The beauty of Morocco had only intensified his clarity, sharpening his instincts for the challenge ahead.

"Enjoy this moment, Rehaan," Kai said, his eyes distant. "Because once we dive back into this investigation, there won't be any time for admiring the view."

Rehaan chuckled, but he knew Kai was right. They were getting closer to the truth, and soon, they would have to face it head-on.

Kai Starling, Ioanna, and Rehaan began their investigation in the heart of Morocco, moving through the vibrant streets of Casablanca. The city was alive with color and history, the air tinged with the scent of spices and the sound of market vendors calling out their wares. But beneath the surface, there was a sense of mystery, as if the city itself held the key to unlocking the secrets of the stolen painting, "The Veiled Mirage."

Their first stop was the famed Hassan II Mosque, a towering masterpiece of architecture. As they marveled at the intricate carvings and ocean views, Kai noticed something subtle but significant: a small inscription near one of the mosaic panels, barely visible, with symbols that matched the ones from the stolen painting. It was their first clue.

"Look at this," Kai said, pointing to the inscription. "It's part of the same puzzle. Whoever stole that painting knew it held more than just artistic value."

Rehaan, standing by Kai's side, raised an eyebrow. "You think this is bigger than a simple theft?"

"I'm certain of it," Kai replied, his voice serious. "The painting is connected to something far older—a secret society, perhaps. We need to dig deeper."

Their investigation led them to meet several key figures, each offering a piece of the puzzle. Mira Al-Hassan, an art historian and expert on ancient artifacts, was their next contact. She explained that the painting had once been in the possession of an ancient order that used art to convey hidden messages, messages that could unlock vast fortunes or powerful secrets.

Later, at the bustling square of Jemaa el-Fnaa, a former security expert named Youssef Rahimi met with them discreetly, sharing intel on the black-market dealings of art and the criminal networks tied to it. He hinted that the painting could be part of a larger game—one that involved some of the wealthiest and most powerful people in the world.

As the investigation unfolded, Kai, Ioanna, and Rehaan began to piece together the motive. The painting wasn't valuable just because of its artistic merit; it was a map—a guide to a hidden treasure or something equally priceless. Whoever held "The Veiled Mirage" controlled access to something much more valuable than money.

The question now was: what exactly was the painting pointing to, and how far would someone go to obtain it?

they moved through the streets of Casablanca, the cool evening breeze carried with it the subtle scent of jasmine and spices. The sun began to set, casting a golden hue over the city, while Kai Starling lit his pipe, taking a deep, thoughtful draw. The smoke curled upwards, blending with the vibrant energy of Morocco around them.

Ioanna, noticing the contemplative expression on Kai's face, smiled softly. "What's on your mind, love?"

Kai exhaled slowly, the smoke swirling around his head like a cloud of mysteries. "This painting... it's not just a treasure map. It's a key to something bigger, something ancient."

Rehaan, walking slightly ahead, paused and turned back to Kai. "Bigger how? Are we talking about a secret society or some hidden fortune?"

Kai took another puff of his pipe and smiled enigmatically. "Perhaps both, my dear Rehaan. Whatever it is, it's powerful enough for someone to go to great lengths to keep it hidden."

The trio found themselves at a cozy café overlooking the Majorelle Garden, the blue hues of the famous landmark reflected in the setting sun. As they sat down, Kai's pipe smoke mixed with the scent of freshly brewed Moroccan mint tea. There was a peaceful moment, a brief reprieve from the intensity of the investigation, as the beauty of Morocco worked its charm on them.

Kai leaned back, his pipe still in hand, eyes narrowing in thought. "Every piece of this puzzle has been hidden in plain sight, as if it's been waiting for the right moment to be discovered."

Ioanna sipped her tea, watching Kai carefully. "You think this moment is now?"

Kai nodded, the soft glow of the café lights dancing in his eyes. "The signs are all around us, Ioanna. We just need to follow the trail of smoke and see where it leads."

With the weight of the case bearing down on them, the sweetness of the moment lingered in the air like the delicate smoke from Kai's pipe, a reminder that even in the midst of danger, there was beauty to be savored.

As Kai Starling, Ioanna, and Rehaan ventured deeper into the narrow alleys of Casablanca, the tension in the air grew palpable. The soft hum of the city's markets faded behind them, replaced by an eerie stillness.

They had barely turned a corner when a group of men appeared from the shadows, their intent clear. "Turn back," one of them warned, his voice cold and threatening. "This isn't your business."

Kai calmly drew on his pipe, taking in the situation with his usual measured gaze. Rehaan tensed at his side, but Kai raised a hand to steady him. "Easy, Rehaan. Let's not give them more reason."

The men stepped closer, forming a loose semicircle around them. Just when it seemed things might escalate, Kai made his move—not with fists or violence, but with words. "Gentlemen," he said, his voice smooth, "we're here for the same reason, aren't we? The painting. Now, we can make this more complicated than it needs to be, or... we can walk away from this like rational people."

The leader of the group narrowed his eyes, momentarily thrown off by Kai's calm demeanor. But before he could respond, Rehaan added with a smirk, "Trust me, you don't want to test us."

The standoff held for a few tense seconds, but then the men backed down. With one final glance, they melted back into the shadows.

Kai exhaled slowly. "See, Rehaan? No need for unnecessary bloodshed."

Ioanna chuckled softly from behind them, "Always the diplomat, aren't you?"

As they walked away, the three of them knew the warning was far from over. The threat lingered, but the fight had been avoided—for now.

Kai Starling, Ioanna, and Rehaan pressed on, their senses alert. The narrow alleys of Casablanca held their secrets well, but Kai's sharp intuition guided them.

They arrived at an old, ornate building, its faded grandeur hinting at a storied past. Kai surveyed the scene with a mix of curiosity and determination. "This place might hold the answers we're looking for."

As they approached, the sense of unease from their earlier encounter lingered. The mysterious men's warning echoed in their minds, a reminder that their investigation had stirred something far deeper and more dangerous.

Inside the building, the air was thick with the scent of history and dust. They began their search, each movement deliberate, their eyes scanning for any clue related to the missing painting. Kai's analytical mind pieced together fragments of information, while Rehaan's experience and Ioanna's insight complemented his efforts.

The search led them through hidden passages and dusty rooms, each discovery adding to the complex puzzle of the painting's disappearance.

The atmosphere was tense but focused, each step bringing them closer to unraveling the mystery.

The chapter ends with the trio finding a crucial lead, a hint that points them toward a new location. As the sun set over Casablanca, the city's shadows seemed to deepen, reflecting the increasing danger of their quest.

As Kai Starling, Ioanna, and Rehaan continued their investigation, the shadow of the earlier threat lingered. They decided to take a break at a small café known for its local charm. The warm glow of lanterns and the aroma of Moroccan spices offered a brief respite from their intense search.

Over mint tea, Kai leaned back, his gaze thoughtful. "We've hit a wall with our leads. Perhaps we need a fresh perspective."

Rehaan, stirring his tea absentmindedly, glanced around the café. "How about we revisit the places we've already been? Sometimes, the smallest detail can lead to a breakthrough."

Ioanna, always perceptive, noticed a man in a dark coat sitting alone at a corner table. He seemed to be watching them, his attention shifting nervously between their table and the entrance.

Kai's eyes narrowed. "Interesting. Keep an eye on him."

The man eventually stood and left the café, slipping into the busy streets. Kai, Rehaan, and Ioanna followed at a discreet distance. The man led them through winding alleys until he entered an old, seemingly abandoned building.

With a signal from Kai, they approached quietly. Rehaan picked the lock on the door, and they slipped inside. The interior was dimly lit, filled with dusty furniture and cobwebs. They crept through the building, the atmosphere charged with suspense.

They finally reached a room where the man was rummaging through a stack of old documents and artifacts. Kai stepped forward, his voice steady but firm. "Looking for something, are we?"

The man jumped, turning to face them with a look of sheer panic. "You shouldn't be here!"

Kai calmly walked closer, his presence commanding. "We're investigating the theft of 'The Veiled Mirage'. You're clearly involved, so why don't you make it easier for everyone and tell us what you know?"

The man hesitated, then, sensing the seriousness in Kai's tone, began to speak. "Alright, alright. I didn't mean to get caught up in this. I was hired to retrieve specific items from the painting's history. I don't know all the details, but I was instructed to keep an eye on anyone investigating the case."

Ioanna, her eyes sharp, asked, "Who hired you?"

The man swallowed hard. "I don't know their name. They go by a code—'The Mantis'. All I know is they have a lot of influence in the art world."

Kai nodded, absorbing the information. "Thank you. This helps us more than you realize."

As they left the building, the city of Casablanca felt more enigmatic than ever. The mention of 'The Mantis' hinted at a deeper conspiracy, one that extended far beyond the stolen painting.

The trio knew they were on the brink of uncovering something significant. The clues were leading them toward a larger network, and they were ready to dive deeper into the mystery.

Back in their rented villa, Kai Starling's demeanor shifted from the casual investigator to one of intense focus. The day's events had left him with more questions than answers, and his mind raced through every detail.

Rehaan and Ioanna watched as Kai paced the room, his expression serious. "We've stumbled onto something bigger than just a stolen painting," Kai said, his voice taut with concentration. "The mention of 'The Mantis' is significant. It's not just a name; it's a symbol of a hidden network operating within the art world."

He stopped pacing and turned to face them. "The clues we've gathered are pieces of a larger puzzle. The stolen painting isn't just a valuable artifact; it's a key to something far more elaborate."

Ioanna, sensing the gravity of the situation, asked, "What's our next step?"

Kai took a deep breath, his eyes sharp and calculating. "We need to understand the connection between 'The Mantis' and the painting. There must be more to this story."

He began to outline his plan. "We'll need to revisit every lead we have, but with a new perspective. We need to look at the painting's history, the people connected to it, and any possible connections to criminal activities."

Rehaan raised an eyebrow. "How do you propose we do that?"

Kai's gaze hardened with determination. "By analyzing every piece of information we have and identifying any patterns or connections. We'll interview anyone who had access to the painting and review any records or communications related to it. Additionally, we'll need to dig deeper into 'The Mantis'. Whoever they are, they're orchestrating this from the shadows."

He picked up a notebook filled with scribbles and diagrams. "Here's what we know so far: The painting was last seen in the possession of Luca Mariani, and its theft was likely orchestrated to obscure its true value. 'The Mantis' is a key player in this, and their motives are linked to something much bigger."

Ioanna and Rehaan listened intently as Kai continued to outline his strategy. The room was filled with a palpable tension as they prepared for the next phase of their investigation.

Kai's meticulous observations and analytical mind were at the forefront of their approach. He knew that every detail mattered and that the answers they sought were hidden in plain sight. With renewed focus, they set their course, ready to uncover the truth behind the painting and the mysterious figure of 'The Mantis'.

The stakes were high, and the city of Casablanca was brimming with secrets. As Kai Starling led the charge, the team was poised to unravel the mystery and confront the shadowy forces at play.

Kai Starling leaned over a map of Casablanca, his finger tracing a route that linked several key locations. The investigation had reached a critical juncture, and every clue seemed to point towards an intricate network of connections.

Rehaan and Ioanna watched as Kai meticulously pieced together the puzzle. "We're getting closer," Kai said, his voice firm with determination. "The trail leads us to a high-end auction house in Casablanca where the painting was once displayed. It's clear now that the painting was not just stolen for its value, but because it's a piece of a much larger scheme."

Rehaan nodded. "So, what's our next move?"

Kai straightened up, his eyes intense. "We need to visit the auction house and see if we can find any leads. There may be records or individuals who can give us more insight into the painting's significance."

Ioanna added, "And what about the people who tried to attack us? Do you think they're connected to this 'Mantis' organization?"

Kai nodded thoughtfully. "It's possible. They might be hired muscle working for whoever is behind this operation. We need to be careful and ensure our next steps don't alert them."

As the team prepared for their visit to the auction house, Kai took a moment to review his notes and make final adjustments to their strategy. The stakes were high, and every decision could impact the outcome of their investigation.

The auction house was an opulent building filled with priceless artifacts and bustling with activity. Kai, Rehaan, and Ioanna entered, blending in with the crowd while keeping their senses sharp. They approached the front desk, where Kai introduced himself as a private investigator looking into the recent theft.

The receptionist, a poised woman named Isabelle Dubois, seemed taken aback but agreed to assist them. "We had a lot of high-profile visitors around the time the painting was last displayed," Isabelle said. "Perhaps some of them can provide the information you need."

Kai and his team were granted access to the auction house's records and were introduced to a few key individuals who had been present during the painting's display. They meticulously combed through documents and engaged in conversations with potential witnesses.

As they gathered information, Kai's sharp eyes caught a crucial detail—a name mentioned repeatedly in connection with high-value transactions and private deals. The name was familiar, but it didn't fully connect until Kai realized it was tied to a figure known only through rumors and whispers: Victor Leclerc, an enigmatic art dealer with a reputation for dealing in stolen goods.

Kai's expression hardened. "Leclerc is our next lead. If anyone knows about the true significance of the painting and the role of 'The Mantis', it's him."

As the team prepared to track down Victor Leclerc, the tension in the air was palpable. Kai's close examination of every detail had brought them closer to unraveling the mystery, and they were on the verge of a breakthrough.

The investigation had entered a critical phase, and Kai Starling was determined to uncover the truth, no matter where it led.

Kai Starling's next steps were deliberate and intense. After uncovering Victor Leclerc's name, he knew that confronting the art dealer was essential to solving the mystery of the stolen painting and the broader conspiracy.

Kai, Rehaan, and Ioanna tracked Leclerc to a lavish mansion on the outskirts of Casablanca. The mansion, surrounded by high walls and security cameras, was a fortress of opulence.

Kai approached with a sense of purpose, ready to make the final breakthrough.

Under the cover of night, Kai's team silently infiltrated the grounds, using their expertise to bypass security measures. They approached a window on the ground floor and slipped inside, making their way through the grand halls of the mansion.

In a dimly lit study, they found Victor Leclerc seated behind a massive desk, his back turned. Kai stepped forward, his presence commanding and authoritative. "Mr. Leclerc," he said, his voice echoing in the quiet room.

Leclerc spun around, his eyes widening in surprise. "What is the meaning of this intrusion?" he demanded.

Kai's expression was steely. "We're here about the painting—'The Veiled Mirage.' We know it was more than just a valuable piece of art; it's a key to something far larger."

Leclerc's demeanor shifted from shock to a calculated calm. "You're quite persistent. But what makes you think you can uncover what I've hidden?"

Kai took a step closer. "Because I've seen the connections, and I understand the stakes. The painting was intended to be a centerpiece in a conspiracy involving powerful individuals. It's not just about art—it's about control and influence."

Leclerc's eyes narrowed. "And what if I told you that the painting was just a part of a larger plan? The real power lies in the people behind it, not the artwork."

Kai's gaze was unwavering. "Then it's time for you to reveal who they are. You've had a hand in this, and now you'll face the consequences."

Leclerc, realizing his position, tried to maintain his composure but was visibly nervous. "You don't know what you're dealing with. The 'Mantis' is a network of powerful players who won't hesitate to eliminate anyone who threatens their interests."

Kai's voice was firm. "Then help us understand the full picture. Provide the information we need, or face the consequences of your actions."

Under the pressure of Kai's unwavering determination, Leclerc finally broke down. He revealed the names of the remaining individuals involved in the conspiracy, the extent of their influence, and their plans. The information was crucial and would bring down the entire network.

As Kai listened intently, he made sure to document every detail. The confrontation with Leclerc had provided the final pieces of the puzzle. With the truth now in hand, Kai, Rehaan, and Ioanna prepared to take their next steps.

The night's events had set the stage for a dramatic conclusion to their investigation. The pieces of the conspiracy were coming together, and Kai Starling was ready to bring the full force of justice upon those responsible.

As the sun rose over Casablanca, Kai Starling, Rehaan, and Ioanna regrouped, their minds sharp and focused. The revelations from Victor Leclerc had provided crucial insights into the conspiracy, but the final pieces of the puzzle were still elusive.

Kai, known for his strategic brilliance, was determined to leverage the information they had gathered. "We're closer than ever to solving this case," he said, his tone resolute. "But we need to be meticulous. The real power behind this conspiracy won't make it easy for us."

The trio set up a base of operations in a secure location, analyzing the data and planning their next moves. They knew the remaining members of the conspiracy were formidable and would be prepared for any attempts to expose them.

Kai's next move was to use the element of surprise to their advantage. He planned a series of covert operations to gather final evidence and confront key players. His strategy involved infiltrating a high-stakes auction where the conspirators were rumored to gather, disguised as potential buyers.

As the auction progressed, Kai and his team observed from the sidelines, blending in with the elite crowd. The atmosphere was tense, with the stakes high and the room filled with influential figures. Kai's keen observations allowed him to identify several individuals who were acting suspiciously, their behaviors betraying their hidden motives.

The pivotal moment came when Kai recognized a familiar face among the bidders—an individual closely connected to the conspiracy's inner circle. Kai's heart raced as he realized this was their opportunity to make a decisive move.

With precise coordination, Kai signaled Rehaan and Ioanna to execute their plan. They discreetly maneuvered through the crowd, positioning themselves to intercept the key figure and gather crucial evidence. The operation was risky, but Kai's meticulous planning paid off.

In a daring move, Kai approached the key figure under the guise of a wealthy investor. His interrogation was sharp and direct, leading the suspect to inadvertently reveal critical information about the conspiracy's final phase and its primary instigators.

The game had indeed changed. Kai's quick thinking and adaptability had allowed him to turn the tables, gaining the upper hand. With the new evidence in hand, Kai and his team prepared for the final confrontation with the conspiracy's leaders.

The atmosphere was charged with anticipation. Kai knew that exposing the full extent of the conspiracy would not only solve the case but also bring justice to those who had been wronged. The final pieces of the puzzle were falling into place, and the resolution was within reach.

Boom!

The sudden explosion rocked the auction house, sending debris and panic through the crowd. Kai Starling, Rehaan, and Ioanna ducked for cover, their hearts pounding as the chaos unfolded around them.

Amidst the confusion, Kai's mind raced. The explosion was a desperate attempt by the conspiracy to thwart their investigation and cover their tracks. But it had only intensified his resolve. He knew they were on the brink of uncovering the final truth.

Through the haze of smoke and dust, Kai sprang into action. He signaled Rehaan and Ioanna to secure the area and ensure their safety while he pursued the escaping conspirators. With the auction house in disarray, the suspects had begun their retreat, hoping to disappear into the city's labyrinthine streets.

Kai's pursuit was relentless. His observations had honed his instincts, guiding him through the chaos with precision. He followed the trail of the fleeing suspects, weaving through the narrow alleys of Casablanca with a determination that bordered on obsession.

As the chase reached its climax, Kai confronted the remaining conspirators in a dramatic showdown. The final confrontation was intense, filled with high stakes and emotional weight. Kai's expertise and bravery were put to the ultimate test as he faced off against the leaders of the conspiracy.

In a climactic battle of wits and courage, Kai dismantled the criminal network, exposing the masterminds behind the elaborate scheme. The truth was revealed, and justice was served. The conspiracy's reign of terror was brought to an end, and the painting, once the object of their greed, was safely recovered.

The dust settled, and Kai, Rehaan, and Ioanna stood victorious amidst the remnants of their final confrontation. The resolution of the case marked the end of a challenging and perilous journey, but it also symbolized the triumph of justice over corruption.

As the sun set over Casablanca, the team knew their work was done. The city's shadows had been chased away, and the secrets had been uncovered. With a sense of accomplishment and a renewed focus on their next adventure, Kai Starling and his team prepared for the future, ready to face whatever challenges lay ahead.

With the final pieces of the puzzle in place, Kai Starling stood amidst the aftermath of the confrontation, the weight of the case lifting from his shoulders. The conspiracy had been dismantled, the perpetrators apprehended, and the stolen painting safely recovered.

Kai looked around at the scene of their victory—broken glass, scattered papers, and the subdued remnants of a criminal empire now rendered powerless. He knew the resolution of this case would send ripples through the criminal underworld, a testament to the efficacy of his team's resolve and skill.

Rehaan and Ioanna joined him, their faces reflecting a mix of exhaustion and satisfaction. The danger had passed, but the significance of their achievement was clear. They had not only solved the case but had also delivered a powerful message: justice, no matter how elusive, would always prevail.

The team took a moment to absorb the gravity of their success. Kai, with his customary pipe in hand, surveyed the scene thoughtfully. He had led them through a labyrinth of deceit and danger, and now, as the final vestiges of tension ebbed away, he felt a profound sense of accomplishment.

"Looks like the case is finally solved," Kai said, his voice filled with a mix of relief and satisfaction.

Rehaan nodded, still catching his breath. "Indeed. And what a journey it's been."

Ioanna, her eyes reflecting the triumph of their effort, added, "The painting is back where it belongs, and the criminals are behind bars. It's a victory worth celebrating."

As they prepared to leave, the sun dipped below the horizon, casting a golden glow over the city. The shadows of the past few days were finally giving way to a new dawn. With their mission complete, Kai, Rehaan, and Ioanna looked forward to their next adventure, knowing that their skills and camaraderie would see them through whatever challenges lay ahead.

The case was closed, but the stories of Kai Starling and his team were far from over. The world was full of mysteries yet to be unraveled, and their journey was just beginning.

As the dust settled from their intense investigation, Kai Starling, Ioanna, and Rehaan gathered in the quiet of their temporary quarters, the weight of their recent success still palpable. Ioanna, curiosity evident in her eyes, turned to Kai.

"Kai, now that the case is closed, can you shed some light on the true motive behind all of this?" she asked, her tone a mix of relief and intrigue. "What was the point of this elaborate scheme?"

Kai nodded, leaning back in his chair and lighting his pipe with a contemplative look. "Certainly. The motive behind the theft of the painting and the orchestrated chaos was much more intricate than it initially appeared."

He began to explain, his voice steady and measured. "The painting, 'The Veiled Mirage,' was not just a valuable artwork; it held secret symbols and hidden messages linked to an ancient society known for its clandestine influence over various criminal enterprises. The theft was orchestrated to retrieve and exploit these secrets."

Rehaan, who had been listening intently, leaned forward. "So, the criminals were after more than just the painting itself?"

"Exactly," Kai confirmed. "The true objective was to gain access to the information embedded within the artwork, which could unlock further secrets and potentially bring immense power and wealth to the group controlling the painting."

Ioanna's eyes widened with realization. "And the attacks and threats were meant to keep us away from uncovering this truth?"

"Correct," Kai replied. "The criminal network wanted to eliminate any interference that could jeopardize their plans. They underestimated our resolve, and that proved to be their downfall."

Rehaan nodded in agreement. "Your observations and deductions were crucial in solving this case, Kai. It's clear now that the stakes were much higher than just recovering a stolen painting."

Kai took a thoughtful puff from his pipe, the smoke curling around him. "Indeed. It was a game of power and deception, and we managed to turn it around. The criminal network's plans have been thwarted, and justice has been served."

With the case concluded and the motive clarified, the team felt a sense of accomplishment. They had not only recovered a valuable artifact but had also uncovered a deeper conspiracy that threatened to shake the foundations of power.

As they prepared to leave Morocco and return to their respective lives, Kai, Ioanna, and Rehaan knew that their journey was far from over. The world was full of secrets and challenges, and they were ready to face whatever came next with the same determination and skill that had seen them through this case.

The adventure continued, with new mysteries awaiting and the promise of future triumphs on the horizon. As the final echoes of their investigation faded, Kai Starling, Ioanna, and Rehaan stood together, the Moroccan sun casting long shadows behind them. The resolution of the case brought a profound sense of closure and accomplishment.

Kai turned to his companions, a satisfied smile on his face. "We've done it. The case is solved, and the secrets of 'The Veiled Mirage' are no longer hidden."

Ioanna and Rehaan exchanged relieved glances, their faces reflecting the triumph of their hard-fought victory. "What an extraordinary journey it's been," Ioanna remarked, her voice filled with gratitude.

Rehaan clapped Kai on the back, a gesture of deep respect. "Your skill and insight were remarkable, Kai. You've outwitted a dangerous network and brought justice to light."

Kai's gaze was steady as he looked at his team. "It was a collaborative effort. We each played a vital role in uncovering the truth. And now, with the case resolved, we can move forward with a clear sense of purpose."

The team's success had not only brought them closer but had also reaffirmed their commitment to their craft. As they prepared to leave Morocco, the memories of their adventure would remain a testament to their resilience and ingenuity.

With one last look at the vibrant landscape, Kai, Ioanna, and Rehaan made their way to the waiting transport. The city of Casablanca, with its rich history and enigmatic charm, would soon become a cherished chapter in their collective story.

As the vehicle carried them toward the airport, Kai took a deep breath, savoring the victory. "Here's to new beginnings and more challenges ahead," he said, raising a metaphorical glass to the future.

Ioanna and Rehaan joined in the sentiment, their spirits high as they looked toward the horizon. The world was vast, and their journey was far from over. The case of the stolen painting had been solved, but the promise of new adventures and mysteries awaited them.

As the sun dipped below the horizon, casting a warm, golden hue over the Moroccan landscape, Kai Starling, Ioanna, and Rehaan stood at the edge of their final destination in Casablanca. The stolen painting, "The Veiled Mirage," had been recovered, and the tangled web of deceit surrounding it had been unraveled.

Kai surveyed the scene with a sense of accomplishment. "The case is closed. We've uncovered the truth behind the painting's theft and exposed those responsible."

Ioanna, her eyes sparkling with relief and pride, nodded. "It's been a challenging journey, but we've made a difference. The painting's rightful place is restored, and justice has prevailed."

Rehaan clapped Kai on the shoulder, a gesture of camaraderie and respect. "Your keen observations and unwavering determination made all the difference. Bravo, Kai!"

Kai smiled, acknowledging his team's support. "It was a team effort. We each played a crucial role in solving this case."

With the case resolved, the trio prepared to leave Morocco. The city's vibrant streets, bustling markets, and rich history would soon be behind them, but the memories of their adventure would remain vivid.

As they boarded their flight, Kai looked out the window, reflecting on the journey. "Here's to new beginnings," he said, his voice filled with optimism. "We've accomplished a lot, but there's always more to explore and more mysteries to solve."

Ioanna and Rehaan shared his sentiment, their spirits buoyed by the success of their mission. The world beyond Morocco was full of possibilities, and they were ready to face whatever challenges lay ahead.

--

Back in London, the familiar sights and sounds of the city greeted them warmly. Kai, ever the picture of calm and collected professionalism, settled into his routine, knowing that new cases would soon come knocking.

One evening, as the rain pattered softly against the window of his office, Kai poured himself a glass of brandy and lit his pipe. He glanced over at Rehaan, who was settling into his own space nearby.

"Is this brandy okay for you, my dear Rehaan?" Kai asked, his tone both casual and curious.

Rehaan took a sip and smiled. "Why not, Kai!"

Kai's face relaxed into a contented smile as he looked out at the cityscape, reflecting on their recent success. "Let's drink brandy and play the violin sometime," he said, savoring the moment. "The adventure may have ended, but the next mystery is always just around the corner."

With that, Kai Starling and his team prepared for the next chapter of their lives, eager for the challenges that lay ahead. The city of London awaited, full of secrets and shadows, ready for the next investigation.

Chapter 6

The Silent Heist Unfolds

The rain drummed against the windows of the dimly lit office as Kai Starling sat back in his chair, the aromatic smoke from his pipe curling around him. He exhaled slowly, his gaze drifting to the stack of books on the table—each one a potential key to understanding the mind of The Fox. The tension in the air was palpable as he contemplated the complexities of their latest case. The stolen documents from The Iron Reserve held secrets that could topple powerful players in London's elite society.

Just then, Rehaan burst through the door, a sense of urgency in his stride. "Kai! You won't believe what I just found out—there's a big case brewing."

Kai raised an eyebrow, setting his pipe aside and picking up a book on criminal psychology. "What have you got?"

Rehaan stepped closer, his expression serious. "The stolen documents. I think there's more to this than just a simple heist. We need to dig deeper."

Kai leaned forward, intrigued. "What do you mean?"

As Rehaan explained the situation, Kai's mind raced, his thoughts intertwining with the theories he'd been reading. The robbery was too clean, too calculated. "Look at this," he said, pointing to the security footage on the screen. "There's something off here. This was no ordinary heist. There's something Bigger."

Ioanna joined them, leaning over to get a better view. "You think it was an inside job?"

"Definitely," Kai replied, his focus sharpening. "The timing was too perfect, and the guards acted too quickly. Someone had to know exactly how the system worked."

Rehaan sifted through the documents, his fingers lingering on a cryptic note found in the vault. "What about this message? It feels like a taunt from The Fox."

Kai's eyes narrowed. "A message left to mock us. It's a game to them, and we need to figure out the rules if we're going to win."

As they delved deeper into their investigation, they decided to confront Marina Hawthorne, head of security for The Iron Reserve. Her access to the vault made her a crucial piece of the puzzle. But something about her demeanor unnerved Kai. He sensed she was hiding something, and her reluctance to cooperate only fueled his suspicion.

Their next stop was a shadowy pub in East London, where they hoped to glean more information about the underbelly of The Fox's network. The air was thick with smoke and whispers, a fitting backdrop for secrets exchanged in hushed tones.

As they settled into a corner booth, Kai resumed his habit of flipping through a book on deception, his eyes scanning the pages even as he listened. "If The Fox is as connected as we think, someone here will have answers," he murmured. Just then, a figure approached—a man with darting eyes, who slid into the seat opposite them.

"I hear you're looking for The Fox," he said, voice barely above a whisper. "You're in over your heads."

Rehaan exchanged a glance with Kai. "What do you know?"

The man hesitated, glancing over his shoulder. "Let's just say, if you're digging too deep, you might find yourself buried."

The warning hung in the air as they pressed him for information, piecing together the network of thieves and informants. But as the conversation heated, the atmosphere shifted. A group of thugs burst through the door, eyes scanning the room before locking onto their table.

"Time to go," Kai said, adrenaline surging. The trio slipped out the back, the sounds of chaos erupting behind them. They ducked into the fog-laden streets, the city alive with danger.

"Who were those guys?" Ioanna asked, breathless.

"The Fox's men," Rehaan replied. "We're getting too close."

Kai's mind raced as they made their way through the winding alleys. "We need to set a trap," he said, formulating a plan. "If we can bait The Fox, we might finally get answers."

Later that night, back at their office, Kai laid out his strategy. "We'll spread rumors about a new set of documents. If we can get The Fox to take the bait, we can draw them out."

As they worked late into the night, tension crackled in the air. The stakes were higher than ever, and the realization that they were now targets only intensified their resolve.

The next day, they executed their plan, carefully feeding information to informants throughout London. They chose an iconic location for the confrontation—a secluded area beneath Tower Bridge, shrouded in mystery and shadows.

As they prepared for the meeting, the sense of foreboding hung heavily. Kai knew that the moment they faced The Fox, everything would change. He could feel the pieces shifting on the chessboard, and he was determined to stay three steps ahead.

Finally, the night arrived. They waited, heartbeats quickening as the fog rolled in. Suddenly, a figure emerged from the mist—a familiar silhouette that made Kai's pulse race.

"This is it," he whispered, steeling himself for the confrontation ahead.

But as the figure stepped into the light, Kai's breath caught. The identity of The Fox was a revelation that sent shockwaves through him, unraveling everything he thought he knew.

As Kai stood beneath the shadow of Tower Bridge, he took a moment to observe his surroundings. The fog curled around the stone pillars like a living entity, hiding secrets in its depths. He felt the weight of the case pressing down on him, the intricate web woven by The Fox becoming clearer yet more confounding with each passing moment.

Kai scanned the area, his keen eyes taking in every detail. A couple of joggers passed by, their breath visible in the cold air, oblivious to the danger lurking beneath the surface. He noted the flickering light from a nearby lamppost, casting eerie shadows that danced across the cobblestones. Every shadow could be an ally or an enemy; every flicker of light, a potential clue.

"Keep your eyes peeled," he whispered to Rehaan and Ioanna, who flanked him. "We need to be ready for anything."

Just then, a figure stepped out of the fog—a tall woman with sharp features and a confident stride. It was Marina Hawthorne, the head of security for The Iron Reserve. She approached with a determined expression, her eyes scanning the area as if assessing potential threats.

"Starling," she greeted, her tone cool but with an undertone of respect. "I hope you have a plan."

Kai leaned against a stone pillar, studying her. "We believe The Fox is connected to the inside job at the vault. You had access—what can you tell me?"

Marina crossed her arms, a slight tension in her posture. "I don't have time for games, Kai. If you think I'm involved, you're mistaken."

"Then help us," he urged, his voice firm. "What can you share about the security team? Anyone acting suspiciously?"

She hesitated, glancing around as if the shadows might be listening. "There have been rumors—strange behavior among a few of the staff. I can't pinpoint it, but I felt something was off."

Kai's mind raced as he pieced together the implications. "Rumors can lead us to the truth. Who should we speak to?"

"Start with Simon Thorne, Edgar's assistant. He's been anxious lately, and his gambling debts are well-known," Marina replied, a hint of concern in her voice. "He might have seen or heard something."

"Thanks," Kai said, noting the lead. "We'll talk to him."

As they moved away from the bridge, Ioanna turned to Kai. "What do you think? Is Marina hiding something?"

"Possibly," Kai replied, his intuition sharp. "But she might be our best chance at finding out who's behind this. Trust but verify."

Their next destination was a small café where Simon Thorne was known to frequent. The air inside was warm and inviting, a stark contrast to the cold outside. Kai spotted Simon seated in a corner, nervously stirring his coffee.

"Mr. Thorne," Kai said, approaching the table. "Mind if we join you?"

Simon glanced up, his eyes darting between Kai and Rehaan. "Uh, sure. What's this about?"

"We're investigating the recent robbery at The Iron Reserve ," Kai stated, studying Simon's reactions. "We need your help."

Simon fidgeted, his fingers tapping nervously against the table. "I don't know much. I just do what I'm told."

"Is that all?" Rehaan pressed. "You were close to Edgar. Did you notice anything unusual before the heist?"

Simon leaned in, lowering his voice. "There was talk of some changes happening at the vault—new security measures, things like that. And then there were strange visitors, people I didn't recognize."

Kai's interest piqued. "Who were they? Did you see their faces?"

"Not really," Simon admitted, his voice trembling. "But they were well-dressed, like they belonged. And one of them… he had a scar on his left cheek."

Kai exchanged a glance with Rehaan, sensing the significance. "We appreciate your help, Simon. Keep your eyes open, and if you hear anything else, let us know."

As they left the café, Kai's mind swirled with possibilities. "A scarred man in high society? That's not a common sight," he mused. "We need to dig deeper into Edgar's contacts."

Later that night, as they reconvened in their office, Kai resumed reading through the books on deception and criminal behavior, looking for patterns and motivations. "Understanding the mind of a criminal is key," he said to Rehaan and Ioanna. "The Fox plays a long game, and we need to anticipate their moves."

Ioanna nodded, her brow furrowed in thought. "What if the connections lead back to Edgar himself? Could he be involved?"

"Possible," Kai replied, contemplating the ramifications. "But we need proof before we make any accusations."

Suddenly, Rehaan's phone buzzed. He glanced at the screen, his eyes widening. "It's Marina. She says she has more information about Simon."

Kai straightened, adrenaline surging. "Let's go. This could be the break we need."

As they hurried out into the night, Kai's heart raced. Each conversation, each observation brought them closer to unraveling the truth behind *The Fox* and the stolen documents. The game was on, and Kai was determined to win.

As the night deepened, Kai Starling gathered his thoughts, the weight of the investigation pressing down on him like the fog that blanketed London. The pieces of the puzzle were starting to align, but he needed to delve deeper into the clues they had uncovered.

Back at their office, he spread out the documents on the table, the flickering light casting shadows over the printed pages. Rehaan leaned against the wall, arms crossed, while Ioanna perched on the edge of a chair, both watching him intently.

"Let's break this down," Kai began, tapping a pen against the table. "We know Simon mentioned suspicious visitors to the vault. We need to identify who they are and what they wanted."

"Marina mentioned changes to security measures," Ioanna added. "What if those visitors were scouting the place?"

"Exactly," Kai replied, scribbling notes. "If they had insider information, they could plan the heist with precision. It wasn't just luck; it was calculated."

Rehaan stepped forward, pulling out his phone. "I'll start digging into Edgar's contacts—see if there's a link between him and anyone with a scar."

"Good idea," Kai said, his mind racing. "But we also need to investigate the security team more closely. If there's an inside man, they'll have left a trail."

Kai leaned back, his thoughts wandering to Marina. "We should talk to her again. She might have overlooked something."

Ioanna nodded. "I'll set up a meeting with her for tomorrow. Maybe she'll be more forthcoming if she feels the pressure."

With their plan in place, Kai focused on the files before him. He began analyzing the security protocols at The Iron Reserve , noting vulnerabilities that could have been exploited. His mind worked like a well-oiled machine, piecing together potential scenarios.

"What about the vault's layout?" he pondered aloud. "If someone knew the timing of the guards and the blind spots of the cameras, they could orchestrate the heist without being detected."

Rehaan, now focused on his phone, chimed in, "I found a list of the security staff. Let me cross-reference their backgrounds. We might find someone with a motive."

As Rehaan typed furiously, Kai's gaze drifted to Ioanna, who was skimming through the notes they'd gathered. Her focus was intense, and he admired her ability to cut through the noise and get to the heart of the matter.

"Any thoughts?" he asked her.

Ioanna looked up, her brow furrowing in concentration. "What if we look at recent personnel changes? New hires might be involved, especially if they were brought in just before the heist."

"Great point," Kai said, writing down another note. "Let's gather information on any new employees or those who left unexpectedly. That could give us insight into who might have been planted there."

The hours slipped away as they worked through the night, poring over documents and sharing insights. Kai's mind was a whirlwind of theories and hypotheses, each one leading him closer to the truth. He felt a growing sense of urgency; the stakes were higher than ever, and time was running out.

Finally, as dawn began to break, painting the sky with hues of orange and pink, Rehaan looked up from his phone. "I found something interesting. One of the security guards has a history of gambling. He might have been in debt, which could have made him susceptible to bribery."

Kai's eyes narrowed. "That's a lead. If he was compromised, he could be our inside source."

"Let's pay him a visit," Ioanna suggested, her voice steady. "We need to confront him and see if he'll talk."

"Agreed," Kai said, adrenaline surging. "We'll go in prepared. If he's involved, we need to be cautious. He could panic and lash out."

As they gathered their things, Kai felt a renewed sense of purpose. The investigation was in full swing, and they were gaining momentum. He would uncover the truth behind The Fox , no matter the cost.

The morning light filtered into the office, Kai Starling poured over the evidence they had collected. With Ioanna and Rehaan at his side, he meticulously crafted a profile of the potential suspect, piecing together fragments of information like a masterful detective.

"Here's what we know," Kai began, spreading out the photographs and notes across the table. "The security guard with gambling debts, combined with Simon's mention of the scarred man, leads me to believe we're dealing with someone who has both inside knowledge and a motive."

He reached for a photograph clipped from a recent article on high-profile criminals. "This is Marcus Leland. He has a history of heists and connections to various underground networks. Look at that scar," he pointed to the image. "It matches the description Simon gave us."

Ioanna leaned in closer, her brow furrowing. "He's notorious. But what's his connection to Edgar or The Iron Reserve?"

"Exactly," Kai replied, flipping through a few more files. "There's a chance he's been working as a hired hand. If Edgar was in financial trouble or needed to dispose of sensitive information, Leland could be the perfect candidate to carry out the job discreetly."

Rehaan chimed in, scrolling through his phone. "I found something. Leland was seen in the vicinity of The Iron Reserve a week before the heist. Witnesses reported a man matching his description loitering around the area."

Kai's mind raced. "That's a significant clue. But we still need concrete proof before we confront him. If he gets wind of our investigation, he'll disappear."

"Do you think he's our inside man?" Ioanna asked, concern etching her features.

"It's possible," Kai replied, uncertainty creeping into his voice. "But I'm not ready to commit to that theory yet. I need more evidence to link him to the robbery."

As they continued their analysis, Kai could feel the weight of doubt settling in. His instincts were sharp, but he couldn't shake the feeling that something was off. Leland was a known criminal, but there were layers to this case that eluded him.

"Let's dig deeper into his background," Kai suggested. "If we can find any connections to the security team or Edgar, we might be able to tie him directly to the crime."

Ioanna nodded, pulling out her laptop. "I'll look into his associates and see if there are any ties to The Iron Reserve."

As they worked, Kai couldn't shake the vision of Leland's scarred face from his mind. He could picture him lurking in the shadows, orchestrating the heist with cold precision. But was he the mastermind, or merely a pawn in a larger game?

"Keep an eye on Marina too," Kai added, still skeptical about her involvement. "If she's hiding something, it could change everything."

Hours passed as they dove into the digital records of Leland's life, combing through social media accounts, financial statements, and connections that might lead them closer to the truth.

Finally, Ioanna leaned back in her chair, her expression serious. "I found a connection. Leland was involved in a similar job years ago—one that went south. His partner in that job was a man named Julian Hart. He's been linked to organized crime in London."

"Another piece of the puzzle," Kai mused. "We need to track down Hart and see what he knows. He might lead us to Leland."

As they prepared for the next steps, Kai felt the familiar thrill of the chase. Yet, beneath that excitement lingered a gnawing doubt. Was Leland truly the mastermind behind the heist, or was there a deeper conspiracy at play?

With determination in his eyes, Kai knew he had to follow this lead, but he remained acutely aware that every move could draw them closer to danger.

"Let's gear up," he instructed, the tension palpable in the air. "We're heading out to find Hart. Time to see if our instincts lead us to the truth—or into a trap."

As Kai Starling, Ioanna, and Rehaan left the office, a chill hung in the air, the streets of London cloaked in an eerie silence. The typical hum of the city seemed muted, as if it too were holding its breath in anticipation of what was to come.

Their destination was a rundown pub in the East End known to attract unsavory characters—an ideal place to find Julian Hart. As they approached, the flickering neon sign above the entrance buzzed ominously, casting an unsettling glow on the damp pavement.

Kai pushed the door open, the creak echoing through the dimly lit room. The atmosphere was thick with smoke and the low murmur of hushed conversations, punctuated by the occasional raucous laugh. He scanned the room, taking in the mix of patrons—faces hidden in shadow, eyes darting suspiciously.

"I'll check the back," Rehaan suggested, nodding towards a narrow corridor. Kai and Ioanna remained near the bar, where a grizzled bartender polished a glass, seemingly oblivious to the world around him.

"Looking for someone?" Kai asked, leaning casually against the bar.

"Depends," the bartender replied, his voice gravelly. "Who are you?"

"Julian Hart. You know him?"

The bartender's expression shifted subtly, eyes narrowing. "Might have seen him. But you didn't hear it from me."

Kai sensed the tension rising, and he leaned closer. "We need information. It's important."

"Important for who?" the bartender retorted, his gaze flicking nervously to the far corner of the bar.

Just then, the door swung open, a gust of wind cutting through the stale air. Kai turned, heart racing as a figure stepped inside—a tall man with a scar running down his cheek, the unmistakable profile of Marcus Leland.

"Shit," Ioanna whispered, her eyes wide.

Leland scanned the room, his expression darkening as he locked eyes with Kai. For a heartbeat, time seemed to freeze. Then, like a predator sensing its prey, Leland's lips curled into a sly grin, and he turned to leave.

"Rehaan!" Kai shouted, snapping out of his momentary paralysis. "After him!"

They bolted through the pub, pushing past startled patrons, but Leland was already disappearing into the crowd outside. The trio sprinted down the street, adrenaline pumping, as they chased after him through the narrow alleyways.

"Split up!" Kai shouted, his voice echoing against the brick walls. "He can't get away!"

Kai veered left, cutting through a maze of streets. He could hear the scuff of footsteps behind him, but he pressed on, determination fueling his pursuit. He spotted Leland up ahead, slipping through a doorway into a shadowy warehouse.

Kai's heart raced as he followed, pushing the door open cautiously. Inside, the air was thick with dust and the scent of something metallic. Dim light filtered through broken windows, creating an unsettling ambiance.

"Leland!" Kai called, his voice steady despite the anxiety bubbling within. "We just want to talk!"

Silence enveloped the space, and the only sound was the creaking of the old building. Kai moved further inside, his instincts on high alert. Suddenly, a loud crash echoed from the back, followed by a faint scuffle.

He rushed toward the sound, his heart pounding. As he rounded a corner, he caught sight of Leland grappling with Rehaan, who was struggling to pin him down.

"Get back!" Kai shouted, charging forward.

In a flash, Leland broke free, scrambling for the exit. But Kai was quicker, lunging forward and tackling him to the ground. They rolled across the floor, dust swirling around them, but Leland managed to kick Kai off and scrambled to his feet.

"Stay away!" Leland yelled, pulling out a knife, the blade glinting menacingly in the low light.

Kai's mind raced. He could see the desperation in Leland's eyes—the man was cornered, and danger radiated from him like heat. "We're not your enemies!" Kai shouted, trying to reason with him. "We want the truth!"

But Leland wasn't listening. With a fierce cry, he lunged toward Kai, who sidestepped just in time, narrowly avoiding the blade.

In that split second, Kai felt a surge of adrenaline. He needed to end this. He swung his arm, knocking the knife from Leland's grip, the weapon clattering across the floor.

Leland's eyes widened in panic, and he bolted for the door once more. Kai was right behind him, pushing through the chaos of the warehouse, his breath coming in quick bursts.

As Leland reached the exit, Kai lunged again, grabbing his collar and yanking him back. They both crashed to the ground, and Kai straddled him, pinning him down.

"Enough!" Kai shouted, his voice raw with intensity. "Who are you working for? What's the connection to Edgar?"

Leland's expression morphed from fear to defiance. "You have no idea what you're getting into!" he spat, his breath coming in quick gasps.

Kai leaned in closer, the weight of their confrontation settling heavily in the air. "Try me."

And just then, a faint sound echoed from the darkness beyond the door—footsteps, growing louder. Someone else was coming.

"Rehaan, Ioanna!" Kai yelled, urgency surging through him. "We need backup!"

As the footsteps approached, Leland's eyes flickered with a mix of fear and desperation. "You don't know who you're dealing with!" he hissed, the threat hanging heavily in the air.

Kai tightened his grip, determined to get answers before it was too late. The tension in the warehouse was palpable, and he could feel the stakes rising—this was no longer just a case; it was a fight for survival.

After the chaotic confrontation with Leland, Kai Starling stepped outside the warehouse, the cool night air hitting him like a wave of clarity. He took a deep breath, trying to shake off the adrenaline coursing through his veins. The city behind him pulsed with life, but he knew he needed a change of scenery to think clearly.

As he made his way through the winding streets of East London, the urban landscape gave way to the outskirts. The towering buildings shrank, replaced by lower structures and scattered patches of greenery. The fog rolled in thicker, weaving through the trees and streetlights, cloaking the area in an ethereal mist.

Kai drove his car down a narrow country road, flanked by ancient oaks that towered overhead, their branches heavy with dew. The gentle rustle of leaves whispered secrets, and he felt the weight of the city lift as he entered a realm where time seemed to slow. The light of the moon peeked through the branches, casting dappled shadows across the pavement.

Rolling hills stretched out before him, painted with the deep greens and earthy browns of the English countryside. Occasionally, he passed charming cottages, their windows aglow with warm light, a stark contrast to the harshness of city life. A small river wound its way through the landscape, the sound of water flowing providing a soothing backdrop to his thoughts.

Kai's mind raced with the clues he had gathered, the pieces of the puzzle swirling together. Leland's warning echoed in his head, intensifying his sense of urgency. He needed to step back, assess the situation from a distance, and connect the dots without the distractions of the city.

He parked near a secluded spot overlooking a valley, where the landscape opened up beneath him. The vastness felt liberating. He stepped out of the car, taking a moment to appreciate the tranquility. In the distance, the lights of London twinkled like stars, but here, surrounded by nature, he could think more clearly.

As he settled onto the hood of his car, Kai pulled out his notebook, scribbling down everything he had observed—the connections between Leland, Hart, and Edgar. The countryside air filled his lungs, grounding him amidst the chaos of his investigation.

But the peace was short-lived. A distant rumble of thunder echoed ominously, and dark clouds began to roll in, casting a shadow over the land. The air felt charged, as if nature itself sensed the storm brewing—not just in the sky, but in the web of deception he was entangled in.

With renewed determination, Kai knew he had to get back to the city, but he would do so with purpose. He couldn't let Leland or anyone else's warnings deter him. The truth was out there, hidden among the shadows, and he was determined to unearth it.

As he made his way back to the car, a sudden flash of lightning illuminated the sky, momentarily revealing the looming threat he felt was closing in. Kai climbed in, heart racing—not from fear, but from the thrill of the chase that lay ahead.

With one last look at the serene landscape, he revved the engine and drove back toward London, the weight of the city awaiting him. But now, he had a plan—a resolve to dig deeper into the mystery that entwined them all.

As Kai sped back toward London, the rain began to pour, drumming against the roof of his car. The streets glistened under the streetlights, reflecting the urgency that now consumed him. The city felt alive, pulsating with secrets waiting to be uncovered.

Arriving at his office, Kai took a moment to gather himself. He entered, drenched but resolute, and spread out the evidence he had collected across the table. Photos of Leland, Hart, and Edgar surrounded a map of the city, dotted with key locations from their investigation.

Ioanna and Rehaan arrived shortly after, concern etched on their faces.

"Kai, we need to talk," Rehaan said, wiping rain from his brow. "What did you find out?"

Kai gestured to the layout. "Leland is connected to a network that's deeper than we thought. The Fox isn't just a thief; he's orchestrating something much larger. Edgar's involvement could be the key."

Ioanna leaned in closer, her eyes scanning the notes. "What's our next move?"

Kai took a deep breath, piecing together the next steps. "We need to confront Edgar directly. If he's linked to The Fox, we have to catch him off guard. I suspect he has a meeting set up soon. We'll use that to our advantage."

They devised a plan, each taking on specific roles. Ioanna would gather intel on Edgar's schedule, while Rehaan focused on surveillance, ensuring they had eyes on every move. Kai would prepare for the confrontation, analyzing the risk involved.

The rain continued to fall outside, mirroring the tension that hung in the air. They worked late into the night, fueled by determination. Each new piece of information only heightened their urgency, and as dawn approached, they felt the weight of the impending confrontation pressing down on them.

With the sun rising, casting a pale light through the rain-soaked windows, Kai gathered his gear. He felt the familiar thrill of the chase—the final investigation was at hand. This time, they wouldn't be caught off guard.

The trio set out toward Edgar's office, a sleek building that stood in stark contrast to the surrounding architecture. As they approached,

Kai's heart raced. He had no idea what awaited them inside, but he was ready to face it.

"Stay alert," Kai instructed, his voice low but firm. "We don't know how deep this goes."

They entered the building, navigating the sleek corridors filled with polished glass and muted conversations. The atmosphere felt charged, a stark reminder of the tension they were walking into.

Kai led the way to Edgar's office, noting the security measures in place. Every instinct told him this was it—the moment of truth.

As they reached the door, Kai exchanged a glance with Ioanna and Rehaan, a silent agreement passing between them. He knocked, and after a brief pause, the door swung open to reveal Edgar, his expression shifting from surprise to calculation.

"Kai Starling," he greeted coolly, stepping aside to let them in. "To what do I owe the pleasure?"

Kai stepped forward, adrenaline surging through him. "We need to talk about The Fox and your involvement in this whole mess."

Edgar's demeanor hardened, the facade of hospitality slipping. "I have no idea what you're talking about."

But Kai was ready. "Leland warned us. Your connections to him run deeper than you're letting on. We know about the documents. They're not just about art; they hold secrets that could unravel everything."

Edgar's eyes flashed, a mix of irritation and fear. "You're barking up the wrong tree, Starling. This conversation is over."

Before Kai could respond, the air shifted. The tension thickened, and suddenly the door slammed shut behind them, locking them in.

"I suggest you leave," Edgar said, his voice cold. "Or things could get very messy."

Kai's instincts flared. "We're not going anywhere until we get the truth."

But as he spoke, a distant sound of footsteps echoed outside, then the ominous clatter of heavy machinery began—reinforcements for Edgar had arrived.

"Time to go," Rehaan urged, already eyeing an escape route.

"No," Kai replied, steeling himself. "This ends now."

The stakes had never been higher. With their backs against the wall, Kai was prepared to confront whatever lay ahead, knowing that this final investigation could change everything.

The tension in Edgar's office was palpable, the air thick with the impending confrontation. Kai felt the weight of the moment pressing down on him, a storm of emotions swirling inside. This was no longer just an investigation; it was a judgment day for all the lies and deceit that had been woven into their lives.

"Step back," Edgar warned, his voice steady but laced with menace. "You have no idea what you're getting into."

Kai didn't flinch. "I know exactly what I'm getting into. You think you can play with lives and get away with it?" Rehaan moved toward the window, glancing outside. "We're not alone, Kai. We need to find a way out before_"

Before he could finish, the door burst open, revealing two burly men flanking Edgar. The atmosphere shifted again, and Kai's instincts kicked in.

"Now, now," Edgar said with a smug smile. "You should have taken my advice."

Without hesitation, Kai's mind raced as he assessed the situation. They were outnumbered, but he had an advantage-knowledge. He had studied Edgar and his connections, and the betrayal in his eyes confirmed his worst fears.

"Edgar, you're a pawn in this game.

The Fox is using you," Kai declared, trying to buy time as he formulated a plan. "You think you're in control, but you're not."

Edgar's expression darkened. "You think you can intimidate me with your bravado? I have powerful allies."

"Powerful allies?" Kai scoffed. "Allies who will turn on you the moment they realize you're expendable."

In that moment, the tension reached a breaking point. Edgar signaled his men to advance, but Kai moved swiftly, adrenaline surging. He grabbed a chair and swung it at the nearest man, sending him crashing into the wall.

Rehaan and Ioanna reacted instinctively, following Kai's lead. The office erupted into chaos, with papers flying and shouts echoing off the walls. Kai fought with purpose, fueled by the knowledge that this was more than just self-defense; it was a fight for justice.

As the struggle unfolded, Kai's thoughts turned to the documents they had uncovered- everything hinged on them. If they could escape with proof of Edgar's treachery, they might be able to dismantle The Fox's network.

But the odds were against them. One of Edgar's men lunged, catching Kai off guard. He grappled with him, their bodies colliding with the desk, sending books and files scattering.

Just as he gained the upper hand, a gunshot rang out, echoing in the confined space.

Time seemed to freeze. Kai's heart raced as he turned to see Edgar standing with a firearm, his face a mask of rage and desperation. "You think you can take me down? I'll make sure you regret this!"

"Put the gun down, Edgar!" Ioanna shouted, her voice cutting through the tension. "This isn't the way!"

But Edgar's grip tightened, his eyes wild. "You don't understand what's at stake! You're meddling in affairs far beyond you."

In that moment, Kai saw his chance.

He needed to appeal to Edgar's fear, to make him realize the

precariousness of his position.

"You're right, Edgar. But you're not the one pulling the strings. You're just a pawn-someone else will take your place when you're gone."

The flicker of uncertainty crossed Edgar's face, and for a brief moment, the resolve faltered. "What do you mean?"

"The Fox doesn't care about you.

You're disposable," Kai pressed, taking a cautious step forward. "This is your opportunity to make things right."

The menacing atmosphere hung heavy, but as the storm raged outside, Kai saw the doubt begin to seep into Edgar's confidence.

"Enough!" Edgar roared, but there was hesitation in his voice.

With a sudden burst of courage, Kai lunged forward, tackling Edgar to the ground, the gun clattering away.

Rehaan and Ioanna quickly subdued the remaining men, their teamwork seamless as they overpowered the intruders. Panting and breathless, Kai turned to Edgar, who lay pinned beneath him, the fear palpable in his eyes. "You can still choose to cooperate. We can expose The Fox together."

Edgar's defiance crumbled as he realized the truth. "I... I didn't know he would go this far."

The storm outside intensified, and Kai knew the final judgment was looming.

They had fought hard to reach this moment, but the real battle was just beginning. They needed to gather the evidence, confront The Fox, and unravel the conspiracy that threatened everythin

As they secured Edgar, the weight of judgment hung in the air. It wasn't just about justice; it was about reclaiming their lives, their integrity, and exposing the darkness that had loomed over them for far too long.

As the chaos in Edgar's office settled, Kai, Ioanna, and Rehaan stood over the subdued man, the reality of their situation sinking in. Edgar's defiance had melted away, replaced by an uneasy acceptance of his precarious position.

Rehaan glanced at Kai, his brow furrowed. "What's the motive, Kai? Why would The Fox go to such lengths to retrieve those documents?"

Kai took a deep breath, piecing together the fragments of their investigation. "The documents hold information that could expose a network of corruption and criminal activity at the highest levels. Edgar thought he was untouchable, but he was merely a pawn in a game of power. The Fox is orchestrating everything, pulling strings to maintain control."

Ioanna crossed her arms, her expression determined. "So, if we expose Edgar, we're not just taking down one man. We could unravel a much larger conspiracy."

"Yes," Kai affirmed, his voice steady. "But it won't be easy. The Fox won't go down without a fight. We need to gather the evidence and prepare for whatever comes next."

Rehaan nodded, his resolve firm. "We can't let fear dictate our actions. If we act now, we can bring the truth to light and protect those who might be harmed by this web of deceit."

As the first rays of dawn began to filter through the windows, illuminating the remnants of their struggle, Kai felt a renewed sense of purpose. The fight was far from over, but they had taken a crucial step toward uncovering the truth.

"Let's gather the evidence," Kai said, his determination evident. "We need to ensure Edgar understands the consequences of his actions. The time for judgment has come, not just for him, but for everyone involved."

With that, they began collecting documents and evidence, piecing together the narrative that would expose The Fox and bring justice to light. The road ahead was uncertain, but united by their resolve, they prepared to face the challenges that lay ahead.

As they left the office, Kai felt the weight of the city around them, aware that the storm was not just outside but within the very heart of London. But together, they would confront it. The truth was their weapon, and they were ready to wield it.

As the first light of dawn crept through the office windows, illuminating the disarray of papers and the remnants of their struggle, Kai stood tall, feeling the weight of the moment. The battle they had fought was not merely physical; it was a clash of ideals, a stand against the shadows that threatened to engulf their lives.

Rehaan turned to Kai, his voice steady and resolute. "This is just the beginning, isn't it? The Fox won't let this go without a fight."

Kai met his gaze, a fire igniting within him. "No, it won't be easy. But we're armed with the truth. And truth is the most formidable weapon we possess."

Ioanna stepped forward, her eyes shimmering with determination. "We have to make sure Edgar understands that he can't hide from the consequences. This isn't just about him; it's about everyone who has suffered because of this network of deceit."

In that moment, Kai felt a surge of unity between them, a bond forged through trials and adversity. They were more than just investigators; they were champions of justice, determined to unravel the corruption that festered in the heart of the city.

With renewed purpose, they gathered the evidence, each document a step closer to revealing the intricate web spun by The Fox. As they prepared to leave, Kai took a deep breath, allowing the gravity of their mission to settle within him.

"Let's be the storm," he said, his voice low but filled with conviction. "Let's unleash the truth and shake this city to its core."

Together, they stepped into the brisk morning air, the rain now a gentle mist that hung in the atmosphere. The city pulsed with life around them, unaware of the reckoning that was about to unfold.

As they walked forward, Kai could feel the anticipation building, the thrill of the chase propelling them onward. The shadows might linger, but they would shine a light bright enough to expose every dark corner.

The game was on, and they were ready to face whatever came next. With every step, they embraced their roles as guardians of truth, determined to confront the darkness and bring the light.

Chapter 7

The Case Unfolds

The soft hum of the overhead lights filled the air as Kai Starling leaned back in his chair, reviewing the latest case files spread across his desk. The office, a cozy space filled with books and mementos from past investigations, was a sanctuary of sorts—away from the chaos of the outside world.

Rehaan leaned against the window, watching the London streets bustle below. "Another day, another mystery, huh?"

Kai chuckled, adjusting his glasses. "You know it. Just when you think you've seen it all, something new comes knocking."

At that moment, the door creaked open, and a woman stepped in, her demeanor a mix of anxiety and determination. "Mr. Starling? I hope I'm not interrupting."

"Not at all," Kai said, gesturing to the chair across from him. "Please, take a seat. I'm Kai Starling, and this is my partner, Rehaan."

The woman, introducing herself as Lydia, sat down, her hands fidgeting in her lap. "I need your help. My sister has gone missing, and the police aren't taking it seriously."

Kai leaned forward, his interest piqued. "Tell us everything."

As she spoke, Kai took meticulous notes, capturing her words with precision. Lydia described her sister's recent behavior— distancing herself from family, strange phone calls, and an inexplicable change in routine. The more Lydia revealed, the more the pieces began to form a troubling picture.

"Have you noticed any specific individuals she's been in contact with?" Rehaan asked, his keen instincts guiding the conversation.

Lydia hesitated, then mentioned a man who had been hanging around her sister's workplace. "She seemed nervous around him. I don't know if he's involved, but…"

Kai nodded, absorbing the information. "We'll need to look into him. But first, let's discuss our fees." He leaned back, his expression serious. "As private detectives, we charge based on the complexity of the case. I assure you, we'll do our best to find your sister."

Lydia nodded, visibly relieved to have their support. "I just want her back."

After finalizing the details, Lydia left the office, her eyes reflecting a mix of hope and fear. Kai turned to Rehaan. "Let's start our investigation."

They began by analyzing Lydia's notes and searching for any connections to the man she mentioned. Hours turned into a flurry of activity—cross-referencing names, tracking social media interactions, and piecing together a timeline of events.

As dusk settled over London, they decided to follow up on the lead at the sister's workplace. They arrived at a small café where Lydia's sister often spent time. The air was thick with the aroma of coffee and pastries, a stark contrast to the seriousness of their mission.

While Rehaan spoke with the staff, Kai's attention was drawn to a table in the corner. There, he spotted a familiar figure—the man Lydia had described. He was deep in conversation, his demeanor relaxed but his eyes darting nervously around the room.

Kai approached cautiously, keen to observe without alerting him. Just then, Rehaan joined him, having overheard a snippet of conversation about a recent conflict involving Lydia's sister.

"Looks like we've found our connection," Rehaan whispered, eyes narrowing.

Kai nodded, formulating a plan. "Let's get closer."

As they moved discreetly, they overheard the man discussing an upcoming event that involved Lydia's sister—a gathering that felt off, filled with coded language and hidden agendas. It was clear now that there was more to the story.

After gathering what they could, they returned to the office, feeling a sense of urgency. Kai spread the notes across the table, analyzing each detail. "The motive seems to be related to something deeper—possibly a rivalry or a hidden secret."

Rehaan nodded, piecing together the family dynamics. "If her sister was involved in something she didn't disclose, that could explain her disappearance."

In the hours that followed, they formulated a plan to confront the man and uncover the truth behind the mystery. With every new piece of information, they felt closer to resolving Lydia's case.

Finally, as night fell, Kai and Rehaan sat back, reflecting on the day's events. "This isn't just a missing person case," Kai mused. "It's a tangled web of family secrets and unspoken motives."

Rehaan smirked, "And we're right in the middle of it. Let's make sure we bring Lydia's sister back home."

With renewed determination, they prepared for the next steps of their investigation, ready to face whatever challenges lay ahead.

Dawn broke over London, Kai Starling and Rehaan gathered their notes, adrenaline still coursing through their veins from the previous night's revelations. The investigation into Lydia's sister was no longer just about a missing person; it was about unraveling a web of secrets that could endanger lives.

"Let's head to the gathering," Kai said, his resolve firm. "We need to confront the man and find out what he knows about Lydia's sister."

They arrived at a nondescript venue on the outskirts of the city, where the event was set to take place. The atmosphere was charged, filled with a mix of anticipation and tension. Kai could sense that something significant was at stake.

"Stay alert," Kai instructed Rehaan as they approached the entrance. "We don't know who we're dealing with."

Inside, the room was dimly lit, with clusters of people engaged in hushed conversations. Kai and Rehaan scanned the crowd, their eyes locking onto the man they'd followed—he was conversing with several others, his body language defensive.

"Let's split up," Kai suggested. "I'll approach him. You keep an eye on the exits."

Rehaan nodded, moving into the shadows while Kai made his way toward the group. As he approached, the conversation shifted, and the man's eyes flickered with recognition.

"Starling," he sneered, his tone dripping with disdain. "I didn't expect to see you here."

"Is that so?" Kai replied, keeping his voice steady. "I'm looking for answers about Lydia's sister."

The man's smirk faded, replaced by a guarded expression. "You shouldn't be poking your nose where it doesn't belong."

Ignoring the threat, Kai pressed on. "I know she's been involved with you and your associates. What do you know about her disappearance?"

"Stay out of it, detective," he warned, taking a step closer. "This isn't your business."

But Kai stood his ground, the weight of his badge heavy in the air. "It became my business the moment she went missing."

The man hesitated, glancing around as if weighing his options. Just then, a commotion erupted near the back of the room—voices raised in anger, a scuffle breaking out. Instinctively, Kai turned, but when he looked back, the man had vanished into the crowd.

"Rehaan!" Kai shouted, rushing toward the disturbance. He found his partner grappling with one of the attendees, who was trying to push past him.

"Help me!" Rehaan grunted, struggling to regain control.

With quick reflexes, Kai intervened, pinning the man's arms behind his back. "What's going on?" he demanded.

"I saw her! I saw Lydia's sister!" the man gasped, panic in his eyes.

"Where?" Kai pressed, urgency in his voice.

"Out by the docks. She was with them—those men!" he stammered, pointing to a group of shady figures lingering in the shadows. "They're dangerous. You need to get her out!"

Kai and Rehaan exchanged a glance, the gravity of the situation sinking in. "We need to move. Now."

They navigated through the crowd, adrenaline propelling them toward the exit. As they reached the door, the atmosphere shifted—the tension palpable. The group the man had pointed out was now watching them closely, their intentions unclear.

"Let's not make this a scene," Kai whispered to Rehaan. "We'll play it smart."

Outside, they hopped into their car, the engine purring to life as they sped toward the docks. The city blurred past them, but Kai's focus was sharp. He replayed the man's words in his mind, determined to find Lydia's sister before it was too late.

Arriving at the docks, they parked the car and scanned the area. The moonlight shimmered on the water, casting eerie shadows. In the distance, they spotted a group of men gathered, their demeanor threatening.

"There!" Rehaan pointed. "That's them!"

"Let's get a closer look," Kai replied, adrenaline surging as they approached stealthily.

As they crept closer, they could hear snippets of conversation—mentions of money, secrets, and a name that sent chills down Kai's spine: Lydia.

With careful precision, they positioned themselves behind a stack of crates, listening intently. "We can't let her talk," one of the men growled. "If she exposes us, it's over."

Kai exchanged a worried glance with Rehaan. They were running out of time.

"On my signal," Kai whispered, readying himself for action. The stakes had never been higher, and they were determined to bring Lydia's sister home.

As they crouched behind the crates, the tension in the air thickened. Kai focused on the group of men, noting their body language—evasive, anxious. It was clear they were hiding something significant.

"Listen up," one of the men barked, his voice low and commanding. "We can't let her get to anyone. If she talks, we're done."

"What about the plan?" another asked, a hint of desperation creeping into his tone. "We need to keep this under wraps until the deal goes through."

Kai leaned closer to Rehaan, urgency igniting his senses. "We have to act now before they make a move."

With a determined nod, Kai signaled for Rehaan to follow his lead. They quietly moved around the stacks, positioning themselves for a surprise confrontation. Just as they were about to step into the open, a sudden shout pierced the night.

"Hey! You can't be here!"

Startled, Kai turned to see a dock worker approaching, eyes narrowing in suspicion. "This is private property!"

"Stay back!" Rehaan warned, raising his hands in a non-threatening manner. "We're detectives investigating a missing person."

The worker hesitated, glancing toward the group of men, who had now noticed the commotion. "You need to leave," he insisted, fear creeping into his voice.

Ignoring the worker, Kai took a step forward. "We're not leaving until we find out what's happening here. Is Lydia's sister with them?"

The worker's expression shifted, revealing a flicker of fear. "You don't understand. They're dangerous. If they see you…"

Before he could finish, the men began to approach, their eyes glinting with menace. "Looks like we've got some nosy detectives," the leader sneered, a cruel smile playing on his lips.

Kai felt the adrenaline spike. "Get ready, Rehaan. We might have to fight our way out."

The men moved closer, surrounding them, but Kai's instincts kicked in. "We're here for Lydia's sister," he called out, trying to maintain some control over the situation. "If you let her go, we'll leave without a fuss."

The leader laughed, a chilling sound that echoed in the night. "You think we'll just hand her over? You have no idea who you're dealing with."

At that moment, a scream shattered the tension—a voice unmistakably Lydia's sister's. It came from a nearby shipping container.

"Get her!" Kai shouted, breaking free from the circle. He and Rehaan rushed toward the container, determined to reach her before it was too late.

The men surged forward, but Kai and Rehaan pushed past them, reaching the door just in time. With a swift kick, Kai broke the lock, flinging the door open.

Inside, Lydia's sister was tied to a chair, her eyes wide with fear. She looked up at them, confusion mingling with relief. "Who are you? Are you here to help me?"

Kai stepped forward. "Yes, we're here to rescue you. Let's get you out of here and Stay quiet!"

Kai ordered, quickly cutting the ropes that bound her. "We need to move."

But as they turned to leave, the leader and his men blocked the exit, anger radiating from them. "You really thought you could just take her?"

The standoff felt electric, the air thick with tension. Kai glanced at Rehaan and Lydia's sister, his mind racing for a way out. "We're not leaving without her," he said, steeling himself.

"Then you'll have to fight for it," the leader sneered, motioning for his men to advance.

Just as the confrontation escalated, a loud crash echoed through the docks. A police siren blared in the distance, growing louder. The men hesitated, fear flickering across their faces.

"Time's up," Kai said, seizing the moment. "Let's go!"

They bolted past the stunned men, sprinting toward the nearest exit as the sounds of chaos erupted behind them. The police sirens drew nearer, the danger closing in.

Outside, they dashed toward their car, Lydia's sister close behind, breathless but safe. "I thought I was done for," she gasped, gratitude flooding her voice.

"Not yet," Kai replied, starting the engine. "We need to get out of here before they regroup."

As they sped away, the reality of what had just unfolded sank in. "What did they want with you?" Kai asked, glancing in the rearview mirror.

"I don't know," she admitted, shaking her head. "I overheard them talking about something big, but I couldn't make sense of it."

Rehaan exchanged a look with Kai, both sensing that this was only the beginning of a much larger conspiracy. "We need to find out what they were planning," Kai said, determination etched on his face.

As they raced through the streets of London, the weight of their recent encounter settled heavily on Kai and Rehaan. Lydia's sister, still shaken, clutched her arms tightly, glancing back nervously as if the men might chase them.

"Where to now?" Rehaan asked, his eyes flicking to Kai, who was focused on the road ahead.

"First, we need a safe place to regroup," Kai replied. "Then we'll figure out what's really going on."

Minutes later, they arrived at a discreet café, its quaint exterior belying the chaos they'd just escaped. Inside, the dim lighting offered a sense of safety, and they settled into a corner booth, still alert.

"Tell us everything you overheard," Kai urged, leaning in closer. "It could be crucial."

Lydia's sister hesitated, her brow furrowing in concentration. "They mentioned a shipment—something coming in soon. It sounded important, and they were worried about it being discovered."

"Shipment?" Rehaan echoed, intrigued. "What kind of shipment?"

"I don't know exactly," she admitted, her voice trembling slightly. "They kept talking about a 'deal' and how it had to go smoothly, or there would be consequences."

Kai exchanged glances with Rehaan, a new sense of urgency igniting between them. "We need to find out what this deal is. If it involves illegal activity, we might have stumbled onto something bigger than we realized."

Just then, a figure entered the café—tall, with an air of confidence that immediately drew Kai's attention. It was a woman dressed sharply, her eyes scanning the room before landing on their table. There was something unsettlingly familiar about her.

"Kai Starling," she said smoothly as she approached, her tone both commanding and alluring. "I've been looking for you."

"Who are you?" Kai demanded, instinctively protective of Lydia's sister.

She smirked, a glint of mischief in her eyes. "I'm Clara Davenport. Let's just say I know a thing or two about your recent… escapades."

Rehaan tensed, ready for anything. "What do you want?"

"I can help you," Clara said, her voice dripping with charm. "You're in over your heads with this shipment business. The people you're dealing with are dangerous, and they won't stop until they get what they want."

Kai narrowed his eyes, skepticism lacing his voice. "Why should we trust you?"

"Because," she replied, leaning in closer, "I'm not just a bystander. I have my reasons for wanting to see this deal fall apart. You help me, and I'll help you find out everything you need."

Lydia's sister glanced between them, uncertainty flickering in her gaze. "What's the catch?"

Clara chuckled softly, the sound both enticing and unsettling. "No catch. Just a mutually beneficial arrangement. You have a missing person, I have information. We can make a formidable team."

Kai considered her proposal, the cogs in his mind turning. "And if we refuse?"

"Then you'll continue stumbling in the dark," Clara replied, her expression unyielding. "And trust me, the darkness is where they thrive."

After a tense silence, Kai sighed. "Alright. But if you're playing games, I won't hesitate to bring you down."

Clara's smile widened, a spark of challenge in her eyes. "Fair enough. Let's start by locating that shipment. I have a contact who might know more."

With a tentative alliance formed, they quickly devised a plan. Clara pulled out her phone, texting her contact, while Kai and Rehaan exchanged wary glances, fully aware of the risks involved.

Minutes later, Clara's phone buzzed. "He's at the docks," she announced. "We need to move—now."

The trio exited the café, urgency driving their footsteps. As they reached the car, a sense of exhilaration mixed with apprehension hung in the air.

"Just remember," Clara said, her tone turning serious, "trust is earned, not given. Keep your eyes open."

As they drove toward the docks, the weight of the night's revelations loomed large. This was no longer just about Lydia's sister; it was a race against time to uncover a dangerous conspiracy that threatened more lives than they knew.

Arriving at the docks, they parked in the shadows, the moonlight glinting off the water. Kai felt a surge of adrenaline as they crept closer to the source of their information.

Suddenly, a loud crash echoed through the area, followed by shouts. Kai's heart raced. "We need to be careful," he whispered, scanning the darkness. "It sounds like something's happening."

As they approached, the scene unfolded—a group of men loading large crates onto a truck, their movements hurried and frantic. Kai felt a chill run down his spine; this was the shipment they'd been looking for.

"Now or never," Kai said, adrenaline surging. "Let's get closer."

With cautious steps, they moved into position, ready to uncover the truth behind the shipment and the people orchestrating it. But as they edged closer, Kai sensed they were not alone.

A figure lurked in the shadows, watching them intently—a silent observer with unknown motives. The stakes were higher than ever, and the thrill of the chase fueled Kai's resolve.

As the dust settled around the docks, Kai straightened up, wiping his hands on his coat. Clara Davenport stood beside him, her gaze sharp, taking in the scene. Even in the chaos, her composure remained unnerved, like someone accustomed to watching the world from the shadows.

"Well, Mr. Starling," Clara said, her voice carrying a calm authority, "looks like you've managed to disrupt something quite significant."

Kai met her gaze. "Significant enough that you're still here."

Clara smirked, but the expression didn't reach her eyes. "I stay where the action is. Besides, this is only the surface. There are far more dangerous games at play."

Rehaan approached, his breath slightly labored from the earlier fight. "The authorities are on their way. But what Voss said back there... it didn't sound like an empty threat."

Kai nodded, his mind already working through the possibilities. "Voss isn't the type to bluff. We've uncovered something much larger than a smuggling ring."

Clara's eyes flicked toward the unconscious men, then back to Kai. "These men work for Edgar Donovan, yes, but Donovan is merely a puppet. The one pulling the strings? That's who you really need to worry about."

"And you know who that is?" Rehaan asked, his suspicion evident.

Clara smiled faintly, her posture relaxed but still exuding power. "I have my suspicions, of course. But as with all things, Mr. Starling, information comes at a price."

Kai raised an eyebrow. "And what exactly is your price?"

She took a step closer, her voice dropping to a whisper. "When the time comes, you'll owe me a favor. Something that can't be refused."

Kai's jaw tightened. Deals with people like Clara were never simple. But he also knew she held pieces to the puzzle they needed.

"Fine," he said after a moment. "But no games. You give us what we need, or the deal's off."

Clara's lips curved into a smile, one that hinted at secrets yet to be revealed. "Consider it a temporary alliance."

Back at their office, the air was heavy with tension. Kai and Rehaan sat across from a new client, a middle-aged man named Mr. Hamilton, who nervously explained the situation.

"My daughter's been missing for days," Mr. Hamilton stammered. "The police—they aren't taking it seriously, but I know something's wrong."

Kai leaned back, his eyes calculating. "And what makes you so sure this isn't just a case of her running off on her own?"

Mr. Hamilton hesitated, glancing between the two detectives. "She was involved with... certain people. Influential people. There were threats—she'd mentioned them to me, but I didn't think it was serious until she disappeared."

Kai exchanged a glance with Rehaan. They had been down this road before—secrets, power, and people who thought they were untouchable.

"I'll take the case," Kai said, scribbling some notes. "My fees are non-negotiable, but I promise you I'll do everything in my power to find her."

Mr. Hamilton sighed with relief, clasping his hands together. "Thank you. Please, bring her home."

The investigation began with a deep dive into Mr. Hamilton's daughter's last known whereabouts. Kai and Rehaan combed through her social media accounts, contacts, and any shady connections she might have had. The clues were sparse at first, but a pattern began to emerge—one that led back to an elite circle of individuals known to Clara Davenport.

Rehaan frowned as he looked over the files. "It's always the same, isn't it? Money, power, people disappearing without a trace. This goes deeper than we thought."

Kai tapped his pen against the desk, thinking. "Clara's connected to this, whether directly or indirectly. If anyone has answers, it's her."

Rehaan leaned back. "So, do we pay her another visit?"

Kai nodded. "But we'll tread carefully. Clara isn't someone to trust blindly. There's always an angle."

As they left their office, Kai Starling's mind was already processing the situation. His gaze drifted around the street, taking in details most people would miss—cracks in the pavement, the faint hum of a distant car engine, the reflection of a figure in a storefront window. It was second nature to him, a skill honed over years of navigating London's underworld.

"Kai," Rehaan interrupted his thoughts, "you think Clara's leading us into a trap?"

Kai's lips twitched into a subtle smile. "Clara always has an angle, but she needs us for something. We're safe, for now."

Rehaan shook his head, "How can you be so sure?"

Kai slowed his pace, his eyes narrowing at the passing faces. "It's in her body language. The way she stood at the docks, the calculated distance she kept. She's testing us, but she's not ready to make her move yet."

Rehaan nodded, taking in Kai's observations. This was why Kai was the leader—his ability to see beyond the surface, to read people like a well-worn book.

As they reached their car, Kai paused, turning toward Rehaan. "One more thing—when she mentioned Edgar Donovan, her voice faltered. Just for a second. She knows more about him than she let on. We need to press her on that next time."

That evening, back at the office, Kai gathered his thoughts while sipping on a cup of tea. Rehaan sat across from him, reviewing the case files. It was in these quiet moments that Kai's leadership truly showed. He didn't demand loyalty or respect—it was given to him naturally because of how he handled the complexities of each case.

"We need to keep the investigation under wraps," Kai said, his tone steady. "Whoever's behind this won't hesitate to come after us if they know we're getting close."

Rehaan nodded. "I'll keep our contacts tight."

Kai stood up, his gaze distant as if piecing together the puzzle in his mind. "There's something we're missing. The missing girl, Clara's involvement, Donovan's connection—it's all linked, but there's a deeper motive we haven't uncovered yet."

Rehaan raised an eyebrow, watching as Kai moved to the window, peering out into the foggy London streets.

"Care to share?" Rehaan asked.

Kai turned, his eyes sharp with realization. "It's about control. Whoever's pulling the strings wants to eliminate those who could expose them—Clara, Donovan, and now us."

Rehaan exhaled. "So what's the plan?"

Kai's voice was firm, yet calm, as he outlined their next steps. "We'll follow the money trail—every transaction, every suspicious account linked to Donovan and his associates. There's always a paper trail, no matter how well-hidden."

The next morning, Kai and Rehaan met Clara Davenport in a high-end café on the outskirts of the city. As they sat at the polished table, Clara gave Kai a knowing smile.

"You've come for more answers," Clara said smoothly.

Kai didn't flinch. "We know about Donovan's financial movements. Care to explain why his accounts are tied to several high-profile disappearances?"

Clara stirred her tea, unbothered by the direct question. "Mr. Starling, you should know by now that the truth is never that simple. Donovan may be involved, but the real mastermind is far beyond your reach."

Kai leaned forward slightly, his eyes never leaving hers. "You underestimate how far I'm willing to go."

For a moment, there was silence. Then, Clara's expression shifted, just enough for Kai to notice. There was something in her eyes—a flicker of uncertainty, perhaps even fear. She wasn't invincible, after all.

Kai's observations had led him to a crucial realization: Clara was playing a dangerous game, but she wasn't the one pulling all the strings. She was a pawn, just like the others.

Kai's eyes narrowed as Clara's subtle shift in demeanor gave away more than she intended. The café was filled with the soft murmur of conversation, but for Kai, time seemed to slow down. He had her where he wanted, and the final blow was imminent.

"You know, Clara," Kai began, his voice calm yet firm, "it's not just Donovan, is it? You're part of this too—whether willingly or because you've been forced into a corner. But the thing is, when people like you get cornered, they start making mistakes."

Clara's hand froze, mid-air, her spoon hovering over her cup. Her confident demeanor cracked for the briefest of moments. Kai could see the gears turning in her mind as she calculated her next move.

"Careful, Starling," she said, her voice as smooth as silk, but there was an edge to it now. "You're playing with fire."

Kai didn't back down. He leaned in, locking eyes with her. "I'm not the one who should be worried. You are. You're running out of time, Clara. The trail we're following—Donovan's dealings, the missing girl—it's all closing in. And when it does, the people you're working for won't hesitate to cut you loose."

Clara's smile faltered, and her eyes flickered, betraying the fear she had been holding back. Kai knew that look. She wasn't invincible. She was trapped in her own game.

Rehaan, watching the tension rise, glanced at Kai. "What's the play here?"

Kai didn't break his gaze from Clara. "Simple. We expose the real power behind this. And Clara's going to help us."

Clara laughed, but it was a hollow sound. "And why would I do that?"

Kai stood, his movements slow and deliberate. "Because if you don't, you're the one they'll come for next. You're already in too deep."

Clara's hand tightened around her cup. For a moment, she said nothing, the weight of her situation settling in. Then, she finally spoke, her voice barely above a whisper. "There's someone else. Someone higher up... far more dangerous than Donovan. If you want to survive this, you'll need to find him."

Kai nodded, his victory sealed. "Who?"

Clara hesitated, but the pressure was too great. She leaned in, whispering a name that sent a shiver down Rehaan's spine.

"Victor Morland."

Rehaan looked at Kai. "That's the name we've been hearing in whispers for weeks now."

Kai smiled faintly. "Looks like we're finally getting somewhere."

Back at the office, the air was thick with anticipation. Kai, Rehaan, and Clara gathered around the table, maps, documents, and evidence spread across its surface.

"The final blow comes tomorrow," Kai said, his voice resolute. "Morland's hosting a private gathering at his estate. That's our only shot to bring this to an end."

Rehaan was already loading clips into his handgun. "We're walking into the lion's den. What's the plan?"

Kai pointed at the blueprints they had acquired. "We'll infiltrate the estate under the guise of guests. Clara will provide access. Once inside, we gather evidence on Morland's operation, then shut him down."

Clara's face remained expressionless, though her eyes flicked between the two detectives. "You do realize that if Morland catches wind of this, none of us are walking out alive."

Kai stood firm, his gaze unwavering. "I'm counting on him to underestimate us."

The next night, the opulence of Morland's estate gleamed under the moonlight as luxury cars arrived at the front gate. Kai and Rehaan, dressed to blend in with the wealthy crowd, stepped out of a sleek black car. Clara followed, her face a mask of cold determination.

The final blow was near.

Inside, the party was a spectacle of wealth and power. Glasses clinked, laughter filled the room, and Morland moved among his guests like a predator among prey, completely unaware of the storm that was about to break.

Kai's sharp eyes caught the subtle glances, the quiet exchanges between Morland and his associates. "It's all here," he muttered to Rehaan. "Everything we need."

Rehaan nodded, his hand brushing the concealed weapon inside his jacket. "We've got one shot at this."

As they approached Morland, Clara suddenly froze, her face pale. "He knows," she whispered.

Kai's pulse quickened, but he kept his cool. "We stick to the plan. No turning back now."

Just as Morland turned to greet them, there was a commotion at the entrance. Armed guards poured into the room, blocking the exits. Morland's cold smile spread as he locked eyes with Kai.

"You really thought you could come here and take me down?" Morland's voice was low, filled with menace. "You've underestimated me, Mr. Starling."

Kai's hand slipped to his weapon as the room grew silent, every guest watching the confrontation. "I've been underestimated my whole life," he said, his voice steady. "But the difference is, I never lose."

In a blur of motion, Rehaan disarmed one guard while Kai pulled the trigger, taking down Morland's right-hand man. The room erupted into chaos, and Kai shouted, "We need to secure Morland now!"

Rehaan sprinted toward Morland, who was trying to escape through a side door. Just as he reached him, Rehaan tackled him to the ground, pinning him down. "You're not going anywhere!"

Morland struggled, but Kai was right behind him, securing Morland's arms. "We have evidence against you, Morland. You're not getting away this time."

With the guards distracted by the unfolding chaos, Kai and Rehaan worked quickly, ensuring Morland was restrained until the authorities arrived. Kai pulled out his phone, calling for backup. The sounds of sirens began to wail in the distance, closing in on the estate.

With Morland secured, Kai and Rehaan turned their attention to finding Mr. Hamilton's daughter, Elise.

"Now that we have Morland out of the way, we should be able to locate her," Kai said. "Clara, do you know where she might be?"

"Yes, I do," Clara replied. "Morland had her kept in a safe house just outside the city. I can take you there."

"Let's go," Kai said, feeling a sense of relief.

They arrived at a small, unassuming building. Clara led the way, knocking on the door. After a moment, it opened to reveal Elise, looking startled but unharmed.

"Thank goodness!" she exclaimed. "I thought I was going to be stuck here forever."

"Not anymore," Rehaan said with a reassuring smile. "You're safe now."

As they helped her out of the house, Kai felt the weight lift off his shoulders. With Morland captured and Elise safe, the case was coming to a satisfying close.

"Let's get you home," Kai said, leading the way.

The end was near.

With Morland captured and the evidence secured, Kai and Rehaan stood on the balcony, the night air cool against their skin. Clara, now a free woman, stood beside them, her expression unreadable.

"Congratulations," she said quietly. "You've won."

Kai glanced at her. "This wasn't about winning. It was about justice."

Clara's lips twitched into a faint smile. "Justice. Yes, I suppose that's what this was."

As she walked away, disappearing into the London night, Rehaan turned to Kai. "So, what now?"

Kai exhaled, a small smile tugging at the corner of his lips. "Now? Now, we rest. Until the next case."

Later that evening, back at his apartment, Kai sat by the fireplace, the soft glow illuminating his thoughtful expression. He poured himself a drink, savoring the quiet after the storm of events. As the flames danced, he couldn't help but muse aloud, his voice steady and confident, "You know, if mystery were a drink, I'd order a double shot of you."

He leaned back, imagining the thrilling possibilities that lay ahead, knowing that the best cases—and perhaps the best connections— were still waiting to unfold.